TAKE ONE TOAD

Take one Toad

with drawings by

RONALD SEARLE

Dennis Dobson : London

Acknowledgements
Transactions of the Folk-Lore Society (1928-1936) Volumes: XXXIX.3; XL; XLI.4; XLIII.1; XLIV.1;
XLV.1; XLVI; XLVII.3.
Primitive Physic: or An Easy and Natural Method of Curing Most Diseases by John Wesley A.M.
(edition of 1780)

ABORTION (Old Norfolk remedy)

Jumping on and off a table for half an hour daily should produce the desired result.

For WHOOPING COUGH (circa 1700)   Let the first man seen sitting on a white horse

be asked what the cure is. What he names is the cure.

For THE HEALTH OF A BABY AT BIRTH

Put a pellet soaked in milk into its mouth. If he spits it out he will die. If he swallows it he will live.

CHILDREN'S HEALTH (Old Norfolk remedy)
Sew them into their clothes in the autumn and don't release them till the spring.

For THE RICKETS (circa 1700)
The child is taken before sunrise to a smithy in which three blacksmiths of the same name
work. One of the smiths bathes the child in the water trough of the smithy. After being

bathed, the young patient is laid on the anvil, and all the tools of the shop are passed one by one over the child, and the use of each is asked. A second bath follows. If a fee is exacted, the virtue of the 'lay' is lost. All three blacksmiths must take part in the work.

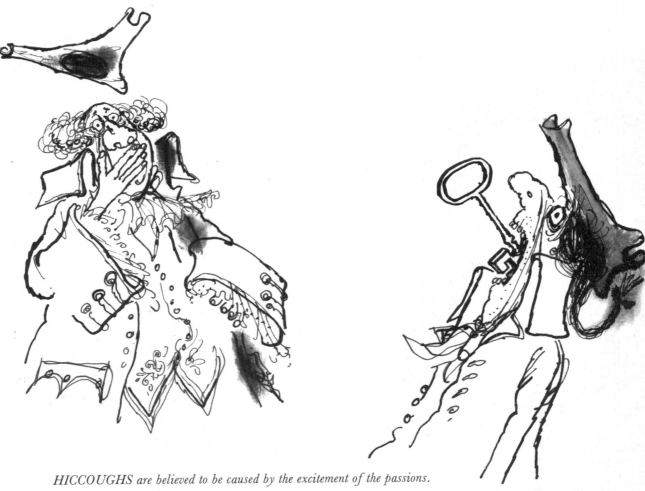

HICCOUGHS are believed to be caused by the excitement of the passions.

If the coughs are convulsive, as often they may become, eat preserved walnuts, and obtain relief.

When you hiccup it means that someone has named you. Utter a name after each hiccup and it will cease when you have named the correct person.

Place your head beneath the desk over which the gospel is being read. If this fails at first another gospel should be read.

Should the sufferer find no immediate way of alleviating his discomfiture he should suppose that it is the result of incontinence and should lie down gently.

These three: the PASSIONS, the RISING OF THE LIGHTS and WIND have caused more than their share of grief.

Parched peas eaten freely have had the most happy effect upon a windy cholic when all other means have failed.

All violent and sudden passions dispose to, or actually throw people into, acute diseases: till the passion that caused the disease is calmed, medicine is applied in vain.

Those less fortunate beings who are subject to the Iliac Passion should hold a live puppy constantly on the belly.

Take small shot in handfuls to keep the heart down.

ERYSIPELAS

The sufferer should fast and then eat the ashes of the sole of the left shoe of another person of the same age but the opposite sex.

BED-WETTING

This can be cured by frying a mouse and having the offender eat it.

For the TOOTHACHE (Seventeenth Century)
Go between the sun and the sky to a ford, a place where the dead and the living cross, lift

a stone from it (the ford) with the teeth and the toothache vanishes.

For the remedy of the TOOTHACHE, which has always been infamous, as much for the discomfiture of the ailment as for the diverse alterations of opinion concerning its relief.

Apply deftly to the aching tooth an artificial magnet.

The suspension of a mole's forefoot from the neck of a child will facilitate the cutting of its teeth.

Firstly ask the name of the sufferer. Then take a hammer and a nail and withdraw behind the woodhouse or some other outbuilding, for the cure has to be effected in secret. When the nail has been driven into a secret place the patient no longer has the toothache.

Teething troubles: Make a necklace of dried deadly nightshade berries. Let the baby wear it and it will prevent the convulsions. Its efficacy can be remarkable.

Gum-ache: The tooth of a man dead by violence will cure a pain in the gums if the sufferer is scarified by it.

EYE INFECTION
For the affection of the eye apply the preparation to the patient's ear.

SORE EYES

Apply dew gathered from roses with a feather.

NOSE BLEED

Get nine people each to tie a knot in a strand of red silk hung about the sufferer's neck. The spell acts better if the knots are tied by persons of the opposite sex.

HEADACHES

For the cure of a headache tie an amulet to the patient's left foot or to his big toe.

Meningitis — Take a young pigeon, split it open from the throat downwards into two equal parts, and apply it outspread to the top of the head, where is should be left for the space of one hour before sleeping. When removed a very strongly offensive odour is emitted and the patient will recover.

The man who suffers from NECK TUMOUR (Anglo-Saxon era)
Let him take neck-wort, and wood-marche, and wood-chervil, and strawberry runners, and
boar-throat, and cockle, and ironhard gathered without iron, 'aethelfarthingwort', and
butcher's broom, and broad-bishopwort and brown-wort. Let him collect all these plants,

an equal amount of each, three nights before summer set in, and make them with Welsh ale into a drink. And then, on the eve of the first day of summer, the man who intends to drink that drink must wake all night. And at first cock-crow let him take a drink once, at first dawn a second drink, at sunrise a third drink. And let him rest thereafter.

WOUNDS: from which all suffer daily.

Bind toasted cheese on a deep cut.

Wash a wound in a to and fro motion, not circular, as the latter motion will induce ringworm, which is not to be encouraged.

A cut will cure quickly and soundly if the weapon (albeit sword, edge of bucket, spike or nail) be well greased.

For a bruise: immediately apply treacle spread on brown paper to induce the pleasantest relief.

For the curing of the WARTS and GROWTHS.

Get someone to buy your warts, and give a half-penny for them . . . then lose the half-penny and the warts will disappear.

Collect as many small stones as you have warts, put them all in a bit of linen and take them to a four cross roads. Stand in the middle of the roads and fling the stones into the air, scattering them to the four winds. The warts will go.

Growths on the nose should be relieved by bleeding. If the bleeding becomes uncontrollable go into a pond or river.

Hard Breasts — Apply turnips roasted till soft, then mashed and mixed with a little oil of roses. Change this twice a day, keeping breast very warm with flannel.

Before Bed.

Against the cramp — Set your boots coming and going when you go to bed.

Unwanted Hair — Two stones under the mattress will ensure the riddance of unwanted hair on the lip and chin.

An Itch — Before retiring to bed wash the parts affected with strong rum.

MALIGNANT SORE THROAT

Take a small frog and, holding it by the hind legs, retain it in the mouth for several minutes. During this time it will suck out the poison, and the patient will recover.

For the treatment of ULCERS, CANCERS, TUMOURS and MALIGNANCIES of an irritating nature.

The laying on of the hand of a corpse is said to give temporary relief.

Persons suffering from ulcerous affections of the mouth — thrush — may be cured by having a person born posthumously blow into their mouths.

To obtain relief for a Cancer in the mouth blow the ashes of scarlet cloth into the mouth or throat. This seldom fails.

DEATH and suchlike afflictions of some severity.

For not allowing death to come and fetch a man: Recite the names of the gods seven times each over all their drawings, and hang the drawings around the neck of the man for whose benefit the charm was made. He will be protected from all misfortune.

For a drowned man: Rub the trunk of the body all over with salt. It frequently recovers them that seem dead.

Affliction of the limbs: At a X-roads artificial limbs should be hung up, that the real ones may be cured.

For THE KEEPING-UP OF SPIRITS

Keep up your patient's spirits by music of viols and ten-stringed psaltery, or by forged letters

describing the death of his enemies; if he is a canon, inform him that his bishop has just died and he has been elected in his place.

AVERTING ILLNESS

Before giving his handkerchief to a friend to wipe his face with, its owner should spit on it in order to avert misfortune or ill-health.

An arm, holding ~~~~~~~~~~~~~~ ~~~~~~~~~~~~ the hole next to my head and shot down the corridor, once, twice, three times. I could hear the spitting sound of the needles hitting the kitchen door.

I still couldn't move. *Help,* I said in my head. *Help.* Malka the Paralyzed in Battle. Roder flinched and closed his eyes.

I raised my blade, saw something, and stuck there, frozen in place. The arm was wearing orange, but it wasn't big enough to be Zul's. He'd sent a sacrifice in his place.

Go. Leave now, I said shakily. *LEAVE.*

There was a cheer from the kitchen.

I still held my blade high, but all by itself the arm fell to the floor, the hand falling open and the gun falling from its fingers. Through the hole in the door, I could see Nothing. We were in translation, and the Forcer's arm was the only part of him that got to make the trip with us . . .

By Delia Marshall Turner
Published by Ballantine Books:

NAMELESS MAGERY
OF SWORDS AND SPELLS

OF SWORDS AND SPELLS

Delia Marshall Turner

A Del Rey® Book
THE BALLANTINE PUBLISHING GROUP • NEW YORK

A Del Rey® Book
Published by The Ballantine Publishing Group
Copyright © 1999 by Delia Marshall Turner

All rights reserved under International and Pan-American Copyright Conventions. Published in the United States by The Ballantine Publishing Group, a division of Random House, Inc., New York, and simultaneously in Canada by Random House of Canada Limited, Toronto.

Del Rey and colophon are registered trademarks of Random House, Inc.

www.randomhouse.com/BB/

Library of Congress Catalog Card Number: 98-93409

ISBN 0-345-42432-8

Manufactured in the United States of America

First Edition: January 1999

10 9 8 7 6 5 4 3 2 1

CHAPTER ONE

The Salute
(*Malka,* Indicating Intent)

The big dark room echoed with the silvery sound of moving feet and blunted weapons striking against each other. Light came in the high windows and got lost in the moving shadows below. All around the circle containing my teacher and me, the students moved back and forth in pairs, dancing with no music, trying to hurt each other. In the center, we stood still, facing one another, teacher and student, surly gorilla man looming over cantankerous monkey girl.

The sword-fighting lessons always began and ended the same way, with a salute. The Sefir Zul, his thick stiff hair standing on end, raised his glittering blade and touched his forehead with the flat, then swept it to one side with a hiss of divided air. I raised my practice sword to my brow in turn and swept it as grandly as if I were bigger than Zul, instead of half his size. I had been studying with the Sefir Zul for three years. *Let me do well,* I said inside my head, as gently as I could.

He did not speak himself, but only began to circle around me. The Sefir Zul never talked much anyway. Following his motion, I stepped sideways, facing him, inside the bouting ring painted on the dark wood floor.

He moved too close and dropped his hand a fraction of an inch too low, as if he were underestimating me, but I wasn't fooled. It was only a standard opening, the Ibrah Kohim, suitable for use against overaggressive opponents. I jerked my hand as if I were about to attack into it, the first variation to the Ibrah Kohim. In response, he pretended to cut at my arm, which would have been naked if I had really attacked. I feigned a flinch, and his real cut came on the other side. I had my weapon back where

1

it was supposed to be, so his sharp edge bounced harmlessly off my bell-guard.

With his height he could have just reached over and whacked me on the head. Or maybe he couldn't; maybe I was good enough to stop him. Or he was lulling me into false security. Or maybe he wasn't.

That was one of the two things I liked best about sword-fighting: the carefully built layers of deception, the strenuous exercise of the mind at high speed, the lightning-fast decisions you had to make. The other thing I liked about sword-fighting was getting to hit people. I rarely got to hit Zul.

He drew back, circling me again. Zul's sword shone in the light. He kept it cleaner than he kept himself. The blade splashed light around the room like honey. Words, cut into the lustrous surface, flowed from the curved guard to the tip. I didn't know what they said. My own sword was a dull gray stick with an imaginary edge painted in white.

I watched everything and nothing, seeing him move smoothly for all his bulk, watching the small shifts in his hand position, feeling the changing angle of his weapon as if it were resting in my own hand, seeing the library of actions scroll past me unrealized.

I lifted my toe a little, as if I were about to make an attack. Zul began to take a half step back, as if he believed me: the first moves of a suite, one I dimly recognized. When my foot came down, he had changed the back step to a forward step and his hand was flying forward, but knowing he would do it, I spun my blade under and around, struck his blade to one side, and thrust my point toward his chest. He danced backward smoothly, pretending to be surprised, but I didn't bother to follow because from the rhythm of his steps I knew it was the fourth Aanandani variation and all the branches that followed from that ended in my defeat. We circled one another again.

He came forward again, light on his feet for such a big man, cutting to my head, but he intended a cut to the side instead. I was there, binding his blade with mine and levering past it to drive point first at his shoulder. He disengaged his blade sharply—

—and we were fighting at twice lesson speed.

We wheeled about each other, stepping in and out, in and out. I could feel my hand flying without thought to take the proper positions in each of the phrases: The Hand-Mihalek, the Meekum, Anthony's Stab, the Sideways Schnell. There was a name for every movement, for every pair of movements, for every combination and rhythm, and he had taught me every one himself. I could hear our blades striking against each other as if we were alone in the room. The Sefir Zul's stiff hair was jerking from side to side. He was red in the face, but then he always was. His hands and feet, as always, moved like those of a man admiring himself in the mirror, but for a change he wasn't watching the other students out of the corner of his eye. He was watching me. He was going to do something horrible again.

Well, I had nothing to lose. With Zul, I was never right, so there were endless possibilities for ways I could be wrong. I decided to try something. I increased the speed again. He followed the tempo change. All of a sudden, I was directing the lesson. He was following my moves. That had never happened before. Well, if I was in charge, I knew what I would do.

Cut, parry, feint, thrust, deceive the blade, step in, pretend to thrust again, and step out. It was a well-worn pattern he had taught me long ago, the Aegyptus. He would believe that I couldn't do anything complicated and go fast at the same time. He thought I was his student, his creation. He wouldn't be the first human to make that mistake.

Cut, parry, feint, thrust, deceive the blade, step in, pretend to thrust, and step out; his face looked bored, and I did it again. The third time, when I moved as if to make the predictable change-cut that was the first variation in the pattern, his blade was exactly where it had to be if he believed my lie, but I wasn't doing the Aegyptus anymore.

He was sure I would be. I had fooled him. So he missed me, because I wasn't there. Instead, I was striking him with a loud whack on the join between his shoulder and his neck. The whack was too loud. I realized the room was silent. His face red with anger—or was it astonishment?—Zul lifted his thick finger to acknowledge the blow, stepping back.

The skin where I had hit him was red, right between the

grimy edge of his collar and the roots of his beard. A welt was already rising. He was going to have a dark blue bruise there, a big one. If I'd had a real sword with a real edge, I would have been looking down at him on the floor. There would have been blood. It was exactly what I had always wanted to do to him.

I was still holding my weapon out, ready for defense, but now I dropped it so that the tip touched the floor. "Sorry, sir," I said.

Then the whole side of my head felt as if it had blown up. He had slapped me with the flat of his blade. He didn't look angry anymore. Now he looked triumphant. "Is your opponent dead, troll girl?" he said with confirmed contempt. "Never drop your weapon until your opponent is dead."

I closed my eyes. Somebody in the back of the room snorted.

Zul went to the tall mahogany cabinet in the back of the room and reached inside. He came out with a neat pile of leather in his huge hands, and a long glittering thing lying on top of the pile. "Go away, Malka," he said, handing it to me. "I can do nothing more with you. You are done."

I took the pile in my arms, staring up at him in rage. He raised his blade and touched his forehead, brought the sword forward, then swept it to one side with a hiss. I put my practice sword in my other hand, lifted the glittering thing from the top of the pile, and swept it grandly back at him, looping it in a final flourish. Somebody else gave a tired laugh. Zul glared around him, the clatter and slide of practice started up again, and a student stepped into the lesson ring and faced the Sefir. As I turned and walked away, I heard him blow his breath out.

He was making me graduate, even though I wasn't done. There was more I wanted to learn.

There wasn't any ceremony besides the clothing. When Zul gave you your armor, whatever grade it was, you were finished. You put it on and went away and couldn't come anymore.

I walked stiffly back to the locker room, stuffed the cotton student armor in the laundry bin, and laid out my new gear to see what grade I had attained. I picked all the pieces up, one by one. I put them all back down, one by one.

This armor was soft, thin, and flexible. It was almost dusty-looking, not so rough it would catch a blade, supple but strong enough to turn a point. The helmet was no more than a cap. The plastron, carapace, and arm-guards were sewn together into a padded jacket with a collar. The leg armor was just trousers. It was armor that said its owner didn't need armor. It was armor just like Zul's, and I knew I deserved it, but there was something fishy. Zul would never grant Sefir rank to anyone if he could help it.

Since I had it in front of me, I tried it on anyway, pulling everything on over my black shirt and skins. The jacket's waist and shoulders fit me exactly. There wasn't anybody else as small as I in the school, so they must be mine. I felt wonderful in it, and I didn't want to take it off.

The sword was long, thin, sharp, and almost weightless. It caught the light with a watery gleam and sent small reflections skittering over the room. The gleaming guard swept over my knuckles when I grasped it, and the grip fit my fingers exactly. When I cut the air, it hissed. I put it in the back-scabbard and drew it a few times, listening to the sliding noise. The mighty Sefir Malka.

I put the cap on, tucked my curly black hair into it, and cocked it slightly. In the middle of the locker room, I stood in the on-guard position, my knees slightly bent, my back straight, my shoulders relaxed, and I drew the blade a few more times, cutting grimly at phantoms. Malka the monkey, fighting back! I could smell the leather. I closed my eyes and shuffled over to the full-length mirror at the end of the locker room, banging into the benches on my way and feeling along the fronts of the lockers. I wanted to surprise myself.

I opened my eyes. There I was. It was a surprise, all right. The surprise was, I was still Malka, still a small maiden with big wide eyes. From the neck down the image in the mirror was a mighty sword-fighter, the way a scale model looks like the real thing. Every detail was perfect, but I looked like a doll in a costume, or a dressed-up cat. At least I didn't have big furry ears and dainty whiskers.

I made a snarling face at myself in the mirror, and laughed. No matter how fiercely I squinted, my eyes were round and clear. Even when I glowered, my brow just crinkled. I felt as if I were scowling, but the scowl looked like a sulk on my rosebud mouth. A Malka doll in a sword-fighting costume. Grr. Ha.

Zul's joke was a nasty one, but if he had given the stuff to me it was mine. I would go wave my sword at him like the performing monkey he obviously thought I was, and then I would march out of the school, I would keep the armor, and Zul could boil his head. I screwed my face up, stuck my tongue out at my image, drew the sword, and strode back into the hall.

And stopped. There, in a perfectly staged scene, was my next-to-worst nightmare.

A man in the orange uniform of a Web Witchfinder, an Enforcer, was standing there talking to Zul.

CHAPTER TWO

The On-Guard Position (*Igor's Crouch*, Facing an Unfamiliar Opponent)

I am not here, I said.

Zul towered over the man like a small mountain. His hair was standing on end again.

"It doesn't do you any good to deny it," said the Forcer, taking a step back with a puzzled expression. Zul's bath habits had that effect on people. The Forcer was another Caliban, of course, a short bland echo of Zul, with quill-like black hair and broad cheekbones. Most Enforcers, Web-wide, were Calibans. The personality was suitable.

"I have no need to protect against witches," said Zul with fine contempt. "You people protect me. Correct?" Only Zul, I thought, would dare talk to an Enforcer that way, but even Zul needed to watch his step.

The Forcer's face didn't move for a moment after Zul's breath hit him. "Correct. Yes. My point exactly," he said finally. "In fact, a witch could hide in the shadow your machine is creating. This is why they are forbidden. So please turn it off and hand it in." He talked in a clumsy, formal way, as if he were reciting. He looked afraid of Zul.

Zul's face didn't change. He didn't repeat himself for his students, and he wasn't going to repeat himself for a government flunky who was interrupting his work.

"You don't understand, sir," continued the Forcer when he realized he had to do all the talking. "There's a huge hole in the flow of magic around your school, a blank spot like a whirlpool. Our detectors are accurate. We know you have a strong magic suppressor."

"You know nothing," said the student who had been taking

7

the lesson after mine, and I didn't even see Zul's hand move, but there was a thin red line on the student's cheek and he was flinching, too late.

"Go look," said Zul to the Forcer, gesturing widely. "No magic suppressor." He turned his back and saluted his student, who sullenly saluted him in turn, the thin red line getting thicker, a red droplet forming at his chin.

Zul was right. There wasn't any machine sucking the magic out of his school. There was a blank spot, though, and it was me. I had better take myself and my blank spot away, and my new sword and armor while I was at it. Time to leave another world. If Enforcement had tracked me down, my long-lost master would be close behind, humming a little tune and carrying a small sharp knife. *I am not here. You cannot see me,* I said carefully inside my head, feeling the thin wash of my words like the last slide of a wave across sand. *Not here.*

The Forcer was still just standing there, as if waiting for a cue. Everybody was still just standing there. I went to the heavy entrance door, and turned the knob. The door opened silently and smoothly. I stepped forward through the widening gap, and I did not run. Very important not to run.

The cobbled street outside was thick with people, as always, and all of them were armed and dangerous, or else just plain dangerous. Zul's was one of ten weapon schools on the block, in a martial arts district, in a city of trained fighters, in a world that provided security guards, soldiers, and Enforcement employees for the whole inhabited Web, all of the Thousand Worlds. I slid into the flow of people walking. Between the shoulders I could see a woman in orange standing beside a gray van. There was a single orange stripe running along its side, and a round logo that said ERC in the center and "Enforcement, Regulation, Control" in neat orange letters around the circumference. It was more serious than I'd thought. The Forcer had brought backup.

The woman moved her head on her neck, peering between the pedestrians. *I'm not here,* I repeated silently, gently—at least gently enough. She obligingly didn't see me. I walked past her, not hugging the building, not moving too close to her, not looking at her, not looking away, not running, fitting in with the crowd.

Behind me, Zul's door thudded open, and there were footsteps above the crowd noise. The Forcer jogged by, swinging his head from side to side to stare at the people he passed. Three gray vans striped with orange bumped past in the road.

"What does she look like?" called the driver of the third van, loudly, leaning out his window. The first Forcer said, just as loudly, "Tiny. Tiny little thing. Short dark hair. Wearing black."

The crowd of people had slowed. They were staring at the vans, and listening to the conversation. All I could see in front of me was shoulder blades. I turned and worked through the mob the other way, trying not to bump into anyone. On Caliban 5, you didn't jostle people. You could get yourself killed. That was one of the reasons I liked it so much here. I always felt safer when I didn't have to pretend to trust anybody. I was going to miss it. I was going to miss the Sefir Zul, smell and all. I was going to miss the hostile, mocking students. I was going to miss my silent days in the school, and my solitary, simple nights.

I stood and breathed at a less busy intersection. Three more gray vans turned the corner and rolled past me, heading back the way I had come. *Don't see me,* I begged, trying to look taller, but their drivers didn't even notice me . . . *The skin where I hit him is red, right between the grimy edge of his collar and the roots of his beard* . . . I had dropped my weapon and apologized for hitting my sword-master. What had happened to me? I had never regretted hurting anyone, ever. No time to think about it.

I walked another block to the subway, and stopped, muttering, *I'm somewhere else* inside my head because in the subway entrance a man was standing at the top of the steps, watching the crowd, holding an instrument in his hand. The patch on his orange jumpsuit read ERC. People went past him down the stairs, not looking at him until they were past. Even on Caliban, it paid to be afraid of Enforcement. Though the Sefir Zul was an exception; I didn't know why.

The Enforcer didn't see me, but I didn't dare go past him. I would have had to bespeak him too *loudly* if I wanted to squeeze past him down the stairs. People noticed if I got too *loud*. I walked past, threading my way among the people. I realized I was walking toward the nearest Web terminal, as if I were a rabbit running down the center of the road in front of traffic. Not a good idea. It would be better to do what I had planned, to go across the continent to the terminal in the next state. They wouldn't be looking for me there. I could slip into the Web and disappear again.

But back behind me I saw another gray van rolling into the intersection. I couldn't go back that way. I shuffled from foot to foot on the corner, then plunged on toward the antiques district. Tobiah might help me. Even if he couldn't, I needed to warn him. All these Forcers couldn't be here just for one little blurry spot in the current of magic. There must have been another conspiracy in the Web, another wiped planet somewhere, and it was tough-on-witches week in the Enforcement head offices again.

The street where Tobiah sold his clocks was full of trees, hedges, and small stuffy stores, their woodwork picked out in dark colors and gold leaf, their windows each displaying one perfect object, usually an antique weapon. Tobiah's shop was an exception; in his window was a great round clock with its face inlaid in Lorimer gweneal-wood, so that you saw the deep patterns in the natural grain before you realized the separate pieces of the inlay formed a mosaic themselves, a bearded face in an armored helmet, with staring eyes and with wrinkles fanning out across the cheeks. I trotted up his stairs and swung the door open.

As usual, Tobiah sat behind the high wooden desk, surrounded in the dimness by softly clicking clocks. His round pale face was calm, his straight wood-colored hair was neatly combed, and his soft nimble hands were folded on each other in front of him. Next to him on the desktop was his familiar spirit. Tobiah's familiar was a clock, of course, a gleaming brass-bound ebony box with brass claw feet and an ivory moon-face. Every witch I'd ever met had a familiar, but every familiar was different, unfamiliar. "Tobiah," I said.

Tobiah didn't stir. He looked through me, or rather he looked at nothing. His smooth face didn't stir. His paper-thin eyelids didn't quiver.

"Hey," I said. Silence. His milky blue eyes regarded some nonexistent spot in the middle distance. Tobiah was always so calm, as if he had all the time in the world. He might have the time, but I didn't.

I cracked the door open behind me. Down in the street, several people were hustling along, looking behind them, and following them came a line of Forcers, turning their heads back and forth, back and forth.

I backed away and let the door close gently. "Tobiah," I said. "Tobiah. Enforcement is on its way. We have to go." Nothing. "Tobiah, *move*," I said, raising my voice and putting force into it.

He blinked.

Tobiah.

His upper lip got sweaty, tiny beads revealing themselves like the mosaic in the gweneal-wood clock.

I waited, but he didn't budge. Paralysis, magic, force field, I didn't know what, but he was frozen. *Tobiah, Tobiah, move,* I said, pulling at his hands. His mouth opened but made no sound, and he fell off his stool. I didn't know if it was my imagination that he looked annoyed for a moment, but when he rolled onto his back, his eyes were still looking into the middle distance, pale blue smudges. A trap, a trap. Tobiah was bait in a trap.

I ran to the back of the store. My sword got stuck in the doorway. I'd forgotten I had it. I had to back up and go through again. I wormed my way through the piles of boxes and old clock cases in the back room, my sword banging into things on either side of me, and found the back door. I wriggled out and slammed the door behind me. *Hidden, hidden.* Behind me a door opened, and there were footsteps, but the alley behind the shops was clear—no, there was a van idling at one end. I scuttled the other way. Three streets over I found myself walking in the direction of the local Web terminal again.

As I walked, my new sword banging against my back and sweat running down my skin under my new armor, three vans came up the hill in a smooth rush, one after another, the orange stripes on their sides flowing past me, the eyes of the drivers fixed ahead of them. I kept walking.

The Web terminal was at the top of a rise, the tops of the main building and the tops of the parked ships peeping above the low sandstone wall that circled the crest of the hill. The entry road to the gate was the only break in the close-cropped lawn surrounding the wall and rolling down to the wide swampy ditch at the bottom of the hill. The agents could see everyone approaching the terminal. There was a glint of light from the slit window nearest to me above the wall.

No one important is coming up the road.

The glint of light flashed out.

I walked through the sandstone gate into the main terminal building. Inside the doors, the station waiting room was crowded, and all the benches were filled with armed people, their luggage piled around their feet. Trained Calibans could get work anywhere on the Web as mercenaries, guards, and martial arts instructors. But there were figures in orange standing at every door. I turned around and a man in orange was moving into place beside the one I had just entered, though he didn't seem to have noticed me. I walked to the other side of the terminal as slowly as I could.

The entrance into the shipyard was a pair of doors with a high stone arch above them, guarded by a Forcer. He stood a few feet before it with his arms folded, looking bored. He was too close to the door, but there was only one of him. *Oh, please move over. Oh, please don't see me.* He unfolded his arms and put them behind his back, rocking back and forth. *Just a little to one side.* He began pacing in front of the doors, still with his hands behind his back, and then while I held my breath he walked over to one side of the doors and leaned against the wall, closing his eyes. *That's it,* I breathed to myself. My whole head felt waterlogged with all the bespeaking. Rivulets of magic surged from side to side behind my eyes. It wasn't good to stir the currents like this. I would have to find a safe place and be still for a week to settle the tides afterward.

I walked up to the doors, past the Forcer. The doors were heavy, but I opened them slowly, and slid through the crack. I eased them shut but let go of them too soon. They thudded gently against each other. I darted to the right, flattened myself against the wall, and froze. *Bump on the wall. Part of the wall.* "Hey!" the Forcer shouted, and he shoved the doors open again, glaring from side to side suspiciously.

"What?" said a woman's voice from the other end of the building.

"Nothing. Could be the midget, could be the wind."

"This is so stupid," she said. "I didn't sign up to play his games. It's all a game to him. Boxes inside boxes inside boxes."

The first Forcer didn't answer, just went inside again. Whose games?

I peeled myself off the wall. I jogged between the lines of parked ships, my scabbard banging on my back and reminding me how sweaty I was. Funky little Malka. I never used to sweat, back when I was smaller. I was changing too much.

Every other ship I passed was Enforcement, with the orange logo painted on the side. I couldn't use those. They had the chilly new killer engines, the black-matter ones you didn't need to be a witch to drive. A black-matter engine would slice me up or blow me away if I walked into it. Even this far outside them, the Enforcement ships made me feel cold when I walked by.

Here was a civilian ship, a white cube with a blue-and-yellow logo. It gave off a warm smell of natural magic. I walked all the way around it, but it was locked, the cargo hatch was closed, and it didn't even have any scratches in the paint. I knocked on the main entrance but nobody came.

I jogged on. Another ship farther down looked less carefully maintained and I had my hopes, but it was locked up, too.

Something quiet drove by in the access lane behind the ships and I saw a flash of gray and orange and the shadow of a head in the driver's seat. *Don't see me.* I had to hurry. This was the most dangerous time, when I was actually at a terminal. This was where the Forcers could catch me, this was where my sharp-smiling master could find me. People kept records at terminals. I jogged on.

After a row of Enforcement jitneys, there was another ship, all angles and shadows. I moved toward it, slowing down as I approached, staring up at it in recognition. When I was little, the houseboat was a fashionable model, and this one looked exactly like the ship my thin-fingered master and I hid on when we left Forest. This one was made of white-painted wood, and it had a porch and shutters, and a paneled front door. The front door had a brass knocker, there was a mailbox next to it, and it looked like someone's weekend cottage.

I walked up to the front door. It was closed, but I put my hand to the knob anyway.

The door swung open in my face. The man inside was just as surprised as I was. He looked down into my face. Then he smiled with delight, a sweet smile. "Come in," he said. He was good-looking in a sad dark way, and very lifelike. His eyes, fringed with astonished black lashes, were the color of river water flowing over white sand. I recognized the model. He had been an expensive android, once upon a time.

He stepped back, holding the door open for me, but I didn't move forward. "Pleased to meet you. I'm Roder Massim," he said. Even his first name was old-fashioned, the name of a cinestar in the first part of the century. People all over the Web named their boys Roder then, but it was a joke name now, a grandfather's name.

I still didn't move. I didn't bespeak him. I was too close, and he would notice.

He held his hand out as if to touch me on the arm, then paused before his fingers reached me. He pulled his hand back and put his arms behind him. Very perceptive. I hated having people touch me. "And you are a witch," he said.

I shook my head. Out of the corner of my eye I could see orange people moving into the open. They were small in the distance, but they were coming.

"Yes, you are," he said. "You are a wandering patch of fog on my instruments. You are a blurry spot in the porch scanner. They are complaining about you on the Enforcement communications channels. I like that. Come in before Enforcement decides to help me with you. I hate it when they're helpful. What's your name?"

He stood waiting, looking polite and sad and clear-eyed. So I did not answer him, but I came in and let him shut the door behind me. Anyway, he wasn't killing me just yet, he didn't smell as bad as the Sefir Zul, and he wasn't my little dead-eyed master.

CHAPTER THREE

The Extension of Blade
(*Blessed Shanahan,*
To Convey Potential Threat)

Inside, it wasn't what I expected. It was dark, shabby, and cool, and it smelled of wood and dry leaves, and of the things that live in old upholstery. The ship I stowed away on so long ago had been bright and very clean, and it smelled of nothing at all.

The floor creaked under my feet. My eyes didn't adjust to the dark right away, because the only light came from the door Roder was already opening for me farther down the hall.

I walked toward him, trailing one hand along the wall of the corridor, which felt smooth and damp. Both walls were plaster-white and lined with wood-framed doors, all closed. Each door had a tarnished brass number on it. Beneath each number was a brass frame, holding a card with a hand-lettered label. The card on the fourth door to the right said ENGINE ROOM, NO ENTRY in faded blue, and I couldn't see any lock on it, but the deep warm smell behind it told me there was a fine big drive there.

The other cards had people's first names on them. It looked like a dilapidated guest-cottage inside as well as outside.

He sucked his chest in so I could get past him into the room. He had on a loose shirt and trousers in a weathered woven fabric, and the top of my head came to the middle of his rib cage. That made him medium height for a man.

"You can stay here. The woman who had it has left," he said, pulling bleached cotton curtains aside and lifting the heavy sash of the window at the head of the bed to let in sunshine and a pale breeze. The bed, the wardrobe, and the chest of drawers were of honey-colored wood. Across the room was a desk of the same wood. The room smelled like starch and soap and pine trees.

The window looked out through the black arms of an enormous pine tree and down a long sloped pasture to a wooded stream. I could see the water flowing, and a crow called from the sky. There was no stream at this Web terminal, no woods, no pasture. I'd never seen a crow on Caliban, or a pine tree.

Roder's ship was bigger on the inside than it was on the outside. You could do that with magic. I did it myself. Magic was indifferent to the concept of space. To magic, everything was in the same place. But it would take a bigger engine than this houseboat should have to maintain this scenery.

He stood with his hands behind his back still, watching me. I supposed he was waiting for me to say something, but I'd said what I had to say, which was nothing at all. He raised his eyebrows. Somebody banged at the front door. He ignored it, but the banging came again. "Excuse me," he said, and walked out, closing the chamber door.

I went to it immediately, but it was locked. I was stuck here.

Footsteps went past in the hall. I knelt on the pillow at the head of the bed and leaned over the windowsill. The branches of the pine tree brushed against the house's walls on either side of me. There was a sky above me, and the ground, a bone-pale carpet of dry needles, was right about where you would expect the ground to be below a first-story window. The wall felt warm in the sunlight and cool in the shadows of the tree branches. Flakes of paint fell to the ground when I brushed them off the wall. This ship looked as if it should be condemned, but an internal space-fold pocket this big would draw enough power from the engine to light a small city.

Enormous power, but no money for repairs to the walls and floors in the corridor, no money for paint.

I leaned farther, looking out. The door clicked open behind me. I pulled back and banged the back of my head and the hilt of my sword on the window sash on the way in.

Roder said from the doorway, "I'm sorry. I startled you. I meant to tell you, don't lean too far out the window. It's too high to reach from outside if you fall. My new employees are always getting stuck outside, and you're shorter than most."

I was his new employee, was I?

A woman squeezed past him in the hall. She didn't glance into the room. Roder left the door open and followed her. Four more people came past, carrying someone whose arms dangled down and whose head dangled back. His head flopped to one side as they passed my room. His eyes were open in his round pale face. He didn't see me. It was Tobiah. He looked dead, and I guessed I would be next, no matter what the android said.

There was only one thing I could do now, what I had always done when I couldn't run instead. I was crouched on the bed with my hand on the hilt of my sword, so I climbed down off the bed and went to the open doorway, drawing the sword as quietly as I could.

"There," said Roder to someone, coming back down the hall. "That's it. Go ahead." Down the hall a door opened and closed, and I could hear his footsteps coming toward my room.

The moment he was within distance, not before, I whipped my new blade around and sliced through him.

Well, I would have sliced through him if he had been there.

Somehow, he didn't finish taking his last step, so I cut through the space in front of him instead, hearing the blade hiss through the air. He didn't look frightened. His face was calm.

When I realized the cut had missed, I took a pace forward, changed the angle of my hand, and swung again. I would have hit him this time if he had stayed where he was, but as I took my step, he drew away, as smoothly as the Sefir Zul. The tip of my sword skimmed the air in front of his shirt, not even rippling the weave.

When I saw the point passing him, and saw him move forward and raise his hand, I was already moving backward, cutting the point of my weapon at the back of his extended hand to make him stop. He didn't stop. Instead, he circled his hand at the last moment and grabbed the flat tip of my sword. His fingers were like a vise.

I struggled with him for an instant, then let go and ran backward down the hall, yanking the front door open. I was facing the backs of two Enforcers on the front doorstep. They started to turn, hands to their guns. I closed the door and put my own back up against it.

Roder hadn't moved. He just stood there with the tip of my sword between his fingers, still calm, still sad and vague. The guard of the weapon bounced up and down, up and down, catching the dim light in the hall.

Roder said, "Here, take it. I don't want it." He paused. "That boy you saw is still alive, by the way, and we weren't the ones who hurt him."

I took one step forward. He didn't move. I took another, and another. When I had my hand on the grip, he separated his fingers. He put his hands behind his back again.

My blade was unsheathed, and he was so close even he couldn't get away if I decided to thrust. Never drop your weapon until your opponent is dead, Malka. We stood facing each other in the dark hallway. I could see his chest rising and falling with his breathing. I didn't know androids had to breathe, though of course they would. They weren't really humans, but they were grown like humans. Besides, I wasn't human either, and I breathed.

Now he looked faintly interested.

I had studied sword-fighting for three years now. I was a professional killer.

Roder was waiting to see what I would do, his fringed sad eyes wider than before.

Please, I began, and then didn't know what to say. I closed my eyes and then opened them again. His expression shifted, as if something had happened, though I hadn't moved, and then he sighed and rubbed his face with both hands and turned away. He hadn't been so sure I wasn't going to kill him after all.

He didn't stick around to gloat. He walked away and went through the door at the end of the hall.

While he was going, I whacked my lovely new sword against the wall next to me, so that little pieces of plaster pattered down on the floor, and I stamped my foot as I did it, and then struck the wall again with my fist, making a wordless noise. What was happening that I couldn't kill an unarmed opponent? I unstrapped the helmet from my head and threw it on the ground. I jumped on it and kicked it. I was going to throw my sword down on the ground and jump on it too, but it was too pretty.

Then I picked up the helmet, dusted it off, and stuck it back on my head. I wiped the dust off my sword with my arm and sheathed it. I strode to the door and flung it open.

He was standing at a counter with his back to me, and he didn't turn around. The room was large and square with a yellow pine table in the center, thick sturdy chairs all around it. A row of china mugs sat on the windowsill, and a gray cat was beside them; it poured itself out the window when I came in. Outside the window was a walled garden, with a stone fishpond in the corner. The thick grass was wild and seedy, and there were pale green vines winding up the stone walls. More space-fold scenery. More threadbare display of power.

I yanked a chair out and sat, scowling.

Roder brought a large steaming bowl over to me, carrying it carefully. It held rice and beans and a thin fragrant red sauce. I stared at the pinhead-sized flowers that floated in the sauce. My head felt empty except for a faint image of my master hunched over a bowl just like this, watching me go hungry while he ate.

He said, "Those flowers are spices. They won't poison you. They're from a world where all the people look like you. Eat up. Then I'll introduce you to the others."

The spices were veronicas, and they didn't grow anywhere anymore, and nobody looked like me anymore, not since Enforcement wiped Forest. Most people didn't know what Foresters looked like. There weren't any of us around anymore and they don't teach the history of wiped worlds. All of us were small, though few as small as I. Foresters were all slight and dark with black eyes and quick hands, and with a taste for the sour veronica in their sweet bean dishes, and all the Foresters were dead, all of them, except for my master who left them all to die.

"Is the sword your familiar?" asked Roder.

Startled, I looked up at him, then at the hilt of my sword. "No. I'm not a witch."

That was enough conversation. I picked up the wide spoon and dipped it into the soup. He had gotten the taste just right, and the texture of the veronicas. I swallowed. He was old enough to have met some Foresters, if I had the year of his manufacture right. I met his eyes and took another spoonful. *Go away and leave me alone,* I urged him.

He smiled and left the room. He knew he had me where he wanted me. He knew exactly how nice the smile was, too, even with all his sadness. Or maybe it was boredom, not sorrow.

The gray cat jumped in and landed on the windowsill again, freezing with her legs bent and her wide eyes fixed on me. There was something about her eyes.

"Hello," I said to her.

The cat hissed back. In words. "Mine," she said. She angled her whiskers forward when she spoke, and moved her mouth in a way that was distinctly uncatlike. She sounded rusty. She was somebody's familiar, starting to fade. Her creator must have died.

"Mine," she insisted.

"Yours," I agreed. "Your ship. Keep it. I don't want it."

I didn't want any of it. I wanted to be able to kill my enemies. I wanted to be a mighty sword-fighter. I wanted to know what that android saw with those eyes. I wanted to know what was going on, and why Enforcement would decide to make me land on melancholy Roder Massim's doorstep. I took another mouthful in the meantime, saluting the room with my spoon. Malka the Mighty, Nemesis of Soup.

CHAPTER FOUR

The Intentional Pause
(*Ram Dass,* For Appraisal
of Opponent)

"Good heavens," said a voice from the kitchen doorway. "So small! How old are you?"

I wiped my chin. The owner of the voice was a woman with an expectant smile, holding a smooth, round pink-nosed animal the size of an orange in her nervous hands. I put my spoon down.

She came in and pulled a chair out, sitting sideways with her knees together, placing the animal on the table and keeping it from running with her hand. Her long dark hair was wound into a multiple knot at the back of her head, making her long oval face even longer. She rippled her fingers over the top of the animal in an odd motion. "Welcome. I'm Electra. What's your name? What's your Talent? What's your story?"

She had white lines tattooed on her neck, too. I kept looking at her until she shifted and leaned back, still moving her fingers restlessly over the smooth surface of the animal. The motion made me want to hit her, or to get up and go to the other side of the room. She was a witch, then, and the animal was her familiar. It blinked at me with eyes pinker than its nose. I blinked back *hello* and it shut them.

"Oh, I'm sorry, I suppose I'm being awfully forward. But welcome to the ship anyway. I'm sure you'll tell us all about yourself when you're ready. Has Roder shown you your room? You can change the decor any time you like, you know, you don't have to stay with it, the ship may be old but it was luxurious in its time. The room used to belong to a very nice girl, a very nice girl indeed," she said with emphasis, though I hadn't contradicted her. Interesting. "Her name was Akamai. She liked the country look, but everyone can't have the same taste, now, can they? You look like you would, let me see, you would like tile floors, and sandalwood furniture, and those lovely old-fashioned grass-mat screens. Am I right?"

My master's house. The feel of cold tile on my bare feet, the aroma of the fragrant wood pervading the house, and the hushed rooms with those soft woven walls and the yellow sand reaching out in every direction outside. I remembered my master's dog Bear, too, his nails clicking on the floor, his yelps when my master pinched him or cut his skin, but she didn't mention the dog. She didn't know. All it meant was Roder had told her I was from Forest. Push, push, she was pushing on me. I could feel it.

"Or perhaps not," she finished amiably. "But I'm chattering on, as usual. What would you like to know? How can I help you? You'll be wanting to know the name of the ship, and what Roder does, and who the rest of the crew is, and why he recruited you, of course—"

How could I stop her? Something that would make her uncomfortable. "Akamai?" I said. The girl who had my room before me, whose name she had said with such false affection.

Her dark eyes went darker, and so did the rest of her face, and her fingers stopped moving for a moment. In the space, I could take a breath. She'd been smothering me.

The cat, still perched on the windowsill, said, "Aaaaaa-kaaaa-maiiii," in a long low call.

"Oh, stop it!" said Electra to it, and it jumped out the window. The woman's mouth was tight, and her fingers still weren't moving.

"Electra, thank you. Let it be," said Roder from the doorway. He stepped in and laid his hand on her shoulder, and she briefly leaned her head against his arm. It made his sad face sadder.

"She asked me about Akamai," she said.

"Ah." He said to me, "Akamai decided to leave the ship without permission. You saw those two when you opened the door? We have an arrangement with Enforcement, but it ends on the outside of the ship. Unless we're on official business."

I waited, evaluating the implied threat, thinking about the way Electra was pursing her lips in disagreement as he spoke. She lowered her eyes. She laid her familiar back in front of her on the table, and fluttered her fingers again. He squeezed her shoulder and let go. "Electra is our interviewer," he said.

Other people began to come in.

The first was a slender boy with a black ponytail. He glanced at me sideways as he came in, not exactly flirting, just sizing me up, a wide-eyed stare like a cat's. An Alcibiadan party-favor just past employment age, he didn't look like any Polytechnic graduate I'd ever seen, but Roder, absently running his fingers over the ponytail, introduced him as "Octavian, our communications officer." Octavian, unperturbed by Roder's caress, ghosted to the table and sat cross-legged in one of the chairs. He continued to watch me as if he thought he must know me from somewhere.

A very tall man with a large head and wide-spaced eyes followed him in, ducking to clear the top of the door. He held a loop of amber beads in one huge fist, and bobbed his head at me kindly. He was definitely a Calypsan priest, one of the People of the Hands. But he was "Cully, our cryptographer," according to Roder, who stroked his shoulder as he passed. Whatever the arrangement Roder had with Enforcement, it let him hire non-Polytechnic witches to run his boat.

They came in the door and Roder, touching each one gently, introduced them and their jobs: Octavian the communications officer, Cully the cyptographer, redheaded Fergus the engineer, brown Pegeen the navigator, toothy Wladyslaw the archivist, gray Julia the cybernalist, and Electra the interviewer with her animal. They were as different from one another as if they'd been taken from their home worlds only the day before.

They all sat around the table, leaving spaces empty, and the room was awash with the warmth of bodies, the creaks of chairs, and the shifting of feet. They were looking at Roder, faces too open and trusting, waiting for something. Electra continued moving her fingers over the skin of her pet, which was bulging its eyes at me.

I felt as if I were struggling to breathe in the thin flood of magic that was drooling all over me. I stood up abruptly, pushed my chair in, and leaned back against the wall. Now they were looking at me instead of Roder, but I didn't care. I didn't want to be a part of that large warm fuzzy group. *Get on with it.*

"Folks, this is our new shipmate," said Roder. "Don't expect her to tell you anything. Electra didn't get anywhere." I heard a couple of inhalations.

"Doesn't look like the Forcers damaged her much," said Pegeen the navigator, whose hair was knotted in furry spirals that made her dark brown skin look like carved wood in comparison. She wore gold-framed eyeglasses. Except for the glasses, which you didn't see much except as jewelry, she looked like an Afrigael businesswoman.

Roder answered for me when he saw I wasn't going to say anything. "Enforcement promised and delivered the young man in the stasis tank, who may or may not be the chronologer we were looking for, and who is certainly damaged. No, this young lady apparently arrived on her own. I only knew she was here because they were talking about her on the channels, trying to track her down. She tells me she's not a witch."

They all laughed, a big warm sound, and I pressed my shoulder blades back against the wall. Nothing more dangerous than the confident innocent. Did he really think I had come here by accident? I'd been herded every inch of the way by Enforcement. Electra squeezed her animal more tightly, staring at me. The animal made a grimace and the pressure increased.

"Don't be frightened," said Roder. "You're safe here."

I bared my teeth at them all. Malka the Savage and Ungrateful Captive.

"Oh, she's not going to tell us anything, I don't know why I'm bothering," said Electra, and let go of the familiar, putting her hands down either side of it while it shook itself and started furiously licking one front paw.

I took a deep breath and sat back down. I was all right now. When witches went to work on me, they sucked the air right out of my lungs, the water right out of my sea.

"I don't know about you people, but I'm hungry," said Cully firmly into the confused silence, and the room slipped into chatter and motion. Roder went to the refectory niche and began handing out platters of food, and the toothy man called Wladyslaw distributed silverware, smiling at me shyly when he gave me mine.

The slim Octavian was still staring at me. He opened his mouth to say something, but Wladyslaw nudged his shoulder and handed him a spoon and the moment passed.

Cully, seated to my right, reached his long arms out to snare a plate, still holding his amber beads in one hand. He offered me a plate of things that looked like tiny rabbit ears, and I shook my head. I laced my fingers together under the table and watched them eat. My armor was hot and uncomfortable, even if it was soft for armor, but that would help keep me alert in this fuzzy cloud of kindness, good food, magic, and interplanetary coziness.

There was a Calypsan and an Alcibiadan, and Fergus, the engineer, was Matrish. I thought Electra was a Murikino. Wladyslaw the archivist had that pale Slavic face with large teeth that could have been Copernican or Szycielist, while Julia could only have come from one of the nontechno prudish worlds of the Gray People. Yet Julia held the highly skilled job of cybernalist, and she was definitely flirting with Octavian, who had forgotten me and watched her with half-opened eyes as if she were wearing a few scraps of glitter. His other arm was draped over the back of Pegeen's chair. He was stroking Pegeen's neck with the back of his forefinger.

It was so rare these days to see so many kinds of people in one room. The Polytechnic training made the government witches in ship's crews into shaven-headed lumps less distinct than a pack of beagle dogs, and most other people stayed home these days unless they had business. People who traveled regularly traveled in families, and carried their worlds with them. The big interplanet shipping consortiums, for instance, were mostly owned by members of the Guese tribes, and passenger lines were owned by the Chemdiah. Accountants and auditors came from Arre-

Catte Waho and wore those stupid crests. And the Forcers were Calibans like the Sefir Zul, pale people with thick quill-like black hair and broad cheekbones, who moved their eyes but not their faces, who had no magic and didn't care to have any, and who liked to hit.

The conversation around the table sharpened from general chatter to a single argument, one that sounded old and well-worn. Pegeen was saying hotly, "Invisibility isn't invisibility unless the light waves aren't reaching your eye at all. I'm sorry if I'm being a purist. If you mean misdirection, say misdirection."

"If you're being a purist, do it right, m'love," said Octavian, his finger still caressing her neck. "The word 'invisibility' just means not perceptible. Not visible. If I can't see it, I can't see it, whether the light is there or not."

"Don't tell me this—" and she vanished from her place at the table and reappeared "—is exactly the same as this," and did nothing I could tell, except for putting her hand to her glasses and letting some tepid magic swirl around her.

"As far as I'm concerned, it is," answered Octavian, still unperturbed. "I can't see you either way, even though I can feel you."

I was puzzled.

"But in this one—" She vanished again but her voice still came from the center of the roiling spell-vortex in the spot she had occupied. "—I am changing the physical behavior of local space, while in this one—" and she reappeared and kept on talking "—I am merely influencing your mind, a much easier task."

"It's what the target sees that matters, not what happens at the source. Either way I can't see you," he said.

"But our visitor can," said Roder from where he sat at the side of the room, not eating. "Can't you, visitor?"

His eyes must have been on me the whole time.

"Can you really?" said Pegeen. "Then what am I doing right now, runt?" and she made a quick gesture at me, one I happened to know because I'd been insulted on Afrigael. I looked away.

"She's blushing," said Octavian with interest. "What did you do, Pegeen?"

"What!" When I looked up again, Pegeen was staring at me and so was everyone else.

"You're an immune?" cried Fergus from the other end of the table. "Martyred Mother's underthings, an immune!"

"You knew what that meant?" asked Pegeen at the same time. "Heavens. I'm sorry. I didn't realize—most people don't—Oh, dear, I apologize."

"But what did you do?" asked Octavian again. "I'd love to be able to make somebody blush like that."

Leave me alone.

Cully cocked his head to one side, looking at me, drawing his beads slowly through his fingers.

"All of you, leave her alone, and watch your mouth, Fergus," said Roder like a preoccupied uncle. Fergus grinned toothily.

A long bell-like tone sounded. Everybody stopped talking. Fergus tipped his chair back and slapped his palm socket to a jack on the counter. "Mennenkaltenei," he said. "Convicted of Class Two offense under the Control Act. Disciplinary action to commence in one hour. Physical wipe."

If they got copies of official communications routinely, their arrangement with Enforcement apparently extended past a little personal privacy inside the ship.

But Mennenkaltenei? With the physical wipe, you got a nice clean planet without any tiresome living things on it. Physical wipe was corrosives. That's what they did to Forest just before I left. Mennenkaltenei must have really annoyed Enforcement now.

Roder's crew didn't believe it, either, and apparently they took it personally. "Mennenkaltenei? The religious planet, the one with the exemption?" Pegeen said, and then she shot out of her chair. "Oh, Lords of Chaos, no!" Abruptly, everybody was cleaning the table. Wladyslaw gave it one last wipe. Fergus, the engineer, had already shouldered Roder aside to get at the engine controls, and the others were turning their chairs around to face the counter. The kitchen was full of people who were used to working with one another, and none of them was looking at me anymore.

I stood up, slid sideways over to the door, and slipped out of the room.

CHAPTER FIVE

The Simple Retreat (*Scuttling Bug*, For Drawing Attack)

No one called after me. I stood in the dark shabby hall and breathed. I hadn't been in a large group of witches like that since I was tiny. Fingers and hands all over one another, ripples of power escaping and fluttering into the room, surges of intention wearing away at my skin.

I went to the end of the hall, past the scratches I'd made in the wall, and opened the front door. The Enforcement guards were gone, but there was nothing at all out there, or rather Nothing with a capital N. We were already in midtranslation, temporarily a dream in the mind of the engine. I'd have to wait until we were somewhere in real space and time before I could escape these lovely fuzzy people.

All the other doors in the hall were locked except for one, and it was the last one I expected to be open. When I put my hand to the knob of the engine room door and it opened, it startled me so much I let go of the knob and the door banged into the wall, but nobody looked out of the kitchen door to find out what the noise was.

Most engine chambers were locked. It wasn't to protect the engine. Engines stayed where they were because they were told to stay. The chambers were locked to protect the passengers. If the crew were the only passengers, though, I guessed they knew enough to stay out of it. I walked into the engine chamber and looked around the room, breathing in. Fergus had called me an immune, but I wasn't immune to magic any more than a fish was immune to water.

The engine chamber was the same size as my bedroom, with

a window in the same place, but otherwise completely bare. Why decorate what nobody ever saw, after all? The average engine was packed with magic, and the human eye was blinded by the blaze. If the particles of magic in here had been normal atoms, I would have been a black hole inside a neutron star, but magic has no mass and takes up little space.

A single light glared from the rough ceiling, the plaster walls were raw and unpainted, and the floor was splintery planks, gray with age. The window looked out into Nothing too. I stood in the center and turned around once, then sat down where I was and closed my eyes. They would never find me here, if they didn't notice the little blurry spot in the middle of their engine.

Any human being except the strongest witch would be melted by a drive. I wasn't a witch. I basked in the impersonal glow. People pushed, but engines were just there. I could taste them at my leisure.

No, I wasn't a witch, but there was a time once when I wanted to be a witch, when I was little. My little master put me on a leash and took me to see the Forest Cybernal, which everybody called the Old Green Brain. It was examination time for a school group of children who had tenth birthdays that week, and we got in line behind them to walk through the outer chamber.

The Forest Cybernal was a real antique of a magic computer from the old days, sealed in a great big globe of solid shielding as if it were radioactive. The children pushed and giggled into the outer chamber, which was narrow and dark with round portholes of foot-thick quartz looking into the vault. Apparently all the children saw a glow coming out of the portholes, judging by the gasps and whoops. I saw no glow. I smelled the dry, blinding heat, and saw magic moving through the big spherical room, which was painted institutional green with dead flies lying around on the bottom. The group of children filed ahead of us, with two shaven-headed Polytechnic cybernalists yelling at them to keep moving.

When everybody came out of the room again, the children chased one another around, some of them pretending the Old Green Brain had talked to them. They thought it would be exciting and dangerous to be a witch and go work for the government, even though they could see how boring the cybernalists were. The cybernalists, meanwhile, were talking in mutters to another staff member, heads down and hands making little irritated movements. "I've never seen the measurement go *down* before," said one of them. "All right, boys and girls, we're going to go through again," she called, and the children, all excited, took twice as long to get in line again. I wished I was with them, but my master yanked my leash and took me with him. When we got home and he measured me and I saw his triumphant expression, I was glad for him that I wasn't a witch. It took a lot to make my master look glad. He wasn't what you would call a warm person. Even when he was hurting me he didn't look happy, he just looked intent.

Something made me open my eyes now. The room looked different. Light was spreading diagonally across the floor. The window didn't look into Nothing now; it looked out over a flat stretch of farmland and a blue-green sky with a blazing yellow sun.

It was outside, it was real, and I could escape.

I was at the window and lifting the sash. It rumbled upward and stuck halfway, though it left enough room for me to squeeze through. I dropped down to the ground. We had landed right in the middle of a field, with plants in neat rows all the way to the horizon. There weren't any buildings in sight. I walked around the back of the ship. Nothing there, either. I rounded the corner to the other side—

—and was tripped, knocked down, picked up by one arm, and dangled in the air.

Cully stood holding me up, showing little strain in his shoulders, but mild surprise in his wide-spaced eyes. "Don't let her go," said Roder, and set off at a run toward the low fieldstone house a hundred yards away.

I hauled myself up by my arm and launched my fingernails at his face, but he grabbed the other hand too. I kicked him. He flipped me upside down and held me by the ankles an arm's length away, and followed Roder at a brisk walk.

Roder was speaking Mennenkalt, calling over and over, "Guardian! Guardian! Come to the door!" but nobody answered. He pounded on the door, yelling, "Come out! Come out! Rot you, Guardian, come to the door!"

"Lord Disorder's panties," sighed Fergus, coming up behind us, his freckled mug flushed and sweaty. Cully lowered me far enough that my head was resting on the ground, though I wasn't carrying much weight on it. When I grabbed his ankles, he kicked me away and held me up again.

Roder backed up, leaned, and rammed through the door with a splintering crash. We could hear him yelling through the house.

"Veremteren koppert," said a thin voice from behind us, and Cully turned around, shoving me behind him for protection. I peered around Cully's side. It was a tired man with a beard and a hat, wearing blue homespun and leaning on a worn wooden stick. He repeated that no one was home.

"Roder!" called Fergus, and began to babble in fractured Mennenkalt so badly pronounced I couldn't make it out. The bearded man shook his head, taking Fergus for an idiot. He made a wiping motion with one hand, then indicated the horizon and the sky. "Go away. No one is home. The Forcers are going to destroy the world in less than an hour. Go away," he said in Mennenkalt.

We were on Mennenkaltenei itself? How had Roder gotten permission to land on a world about to undergo a Class Two wipe?

Roder burst out onto the porch and ran toward the bearded man, who began to repeat what he'd said once again as he watched the android approach.

"You know about the Enforcement action?" said Roder.

The man shrugged. He nodded.

"We can't talk here. It's about to happen. Please come with us," said the android.

The Mennenkalt looked annoyed and shook his head.

Roder lifted his hand. Something sparkled in it. He hit the man's shoulder with it, and the native looked surprised, and then even more surprised, and then his eyes rolled up in his head. The sparkling thing had been a stunner. He slumped forward, and Roder ducked under him as he did and stood up with the man draped over his shoulders. "Fifteen minutes," he said, and everybody ran.

Cully dropped me once we were in the front door of the ship, and I rolled to my knees, rubbing my head. Fergus and Roder ran down the hall, while Cully made me get up and shooed me ahead of him. "How ever did you get out by yourself, spider? You need a baby-sitter. You could have had your chowder boiled for sure," he said. "That planet is about to get cleaned off, and everything living with it." He hustled me ahead of him into the kitchen and made me sit against the wall.

"Let's go, let's go," Roder was saying over and over, and Fergus, with his palm socket already on the plug, was shaking his head.

"Something's wrong with the engine. It's complaining about a draft. It says it's cold."

"If we don't get out in five minutes, we're dead," said Roder.

Fergus was rubbing his head. "It says there's a hole."

"Oh!" I said, and got up. Cully casually put his arm across the doorway to stop me from leaving. "I left the window open in the engine room," I said to him. He stared. I repeated, "I left the window—"

"Go, let her go, go!" shouted Roder, and I slipped under Cully's arm and ran down the hall and into the engine chamber. I hauled at the sash. It was still stuck halfway, and I couldn't jiggle it loose. I reached up to the top of the panel and hung my whole weight on it. *Please shut, please shut,* I muttered to myself, and I heard a grinding noise, but it stopped. *Shut, shut, shut,* I chanted to myself, and it stuttered down inch by inch until it slammed.

Cully was at the door. "Okay, go," I said, but he couldn't hear me. He couldn't see me, either. He was blinded by the light of the engine. I ran across the room, pushed him out of the doorway, shut the door, and said, "Okay. You can go."

He turned and called, "Go ahead," to the people in the kitchen. Then he grabbed my arm and began to shove me down the corridor. "You walked into the engine room, waltzed through the engine, and jumped out the flaming window, just like that, did you, squirrel girl?" he said, giving me a push.

I broke away, ran three steps, whirled, drew my blade, and met him with its point squarely in the center of his chest just in time for him to stop. "Don't push me," I said, stamping my foot. "Don't yank me, don't drag me, don't throw me, *don't touch me*. Don't ever touch me again." I pleaded silently for him not to notice I wasn't pushing the weapon in. What was happening to me?

"If you don't climb into the engine chamber again, I won't," he said, not moving. He had a small dark red spot where the point had gone through the fabric. I was glad he hadn't moved closer, and ashamed that I was glad. I yanked the sword away and smacked the wall with it. I glared at him, breathing hard, but he didn't look at me.

"Aaah!" I said, and kicked the wall, and stormed ahead of him into the kitchen.

Nobody paid any attention when I came in. Slender black-haired Octavian the communications officer was apparently having an epileptic attack, with Roder and everybody else watching him. Octavian's teeth were bared, his dark eyes were slits, his back was arched, and his whole body was vibrating so that the black pendant he wore bounced on his chest. The Mennenkalt was out cold on the floor, his hands folded over his staff and his hat to one side.

"Mmmm!" said Octavian with vulgar satisfaction, and opened his black-lined eyes wide. He was still vibrating.

"NeverMind?" inquired Roder.

"NeverNeverNeverMind," answered Octavian in a deep voice not his own. He was one remarkable communications officer if he could reach the Web Center Cybernal all by himself.

Roder began talking rapidly. "Monitor Roder Massim filing Petition of Appeal against the Office of Enforcement, Regulation, and Control, requesting stay of disciplinary action against Mennenkaltenei for Class Two offense against the Control Act, reason insufficient notice to Monitor of action, absence of due process, endangerment of public safety, violation of civil rights, hindrance of government officials— Pegeen, am I missing anything?"

"Wasting public funds," said Pegeen. "Looking ugly, kicking puppies, and spitting on the sidewalk. You really going to put civil rights in there?"

"—and wasting public funds," he finished. "NeverMind?"

Octavian rolled his eyes. "It's thinking," he said in his normal voice. "If you can call it thinking." Then he shuddered and said in the deep voice of the NeverMind, "Petition of Appeal filed, thirty-day stay awarded, all evidence must be presented by then. Web Center Cybernal has spoken. Ouch," he finished in his normal voice and rubbed his arms. "Completely insane."

"The larger the Mind, the loonier," said Cully tritely.

"No, the NeverMind's getting worse. Really." Octavian's voice was remote, and his eyes were watering. "And you are so noisy," he said to me. "Be quiet when I'm trying to listen."

I set my jaw, but nobody was listening to him now. "Thirty days, folks," said Roder. "Thirty days. Pegeen, I'm willing to bet the Mennenkalts didn't do anything serious. They're not like that. I can get Enforcement on the failure to file notice, but the most important part of the charge is violation of civil rights. I think we're finally going to get them with that one."

There was a dead silence. Cully nodded kindly, passing his beads through his fingers.

"Thirty days," repeated the android. "Cully, you have a stain on your shirt."

"The new girl poked me with her sticker thing," the Calypsan answered, and everybody turned around and looked at me as if it were easier than looking at Roder.

"Cranky little sprat," said Octavian.

"Malka," I said. Roder raised his eyebrows.

The bell-like tone sounded again, and Fergus went over to the palm socket.

"I'm not a sprat. I'm not a squirrel, or a spider, either. My name is Malka," I repeated, sticking my chin out, but Fergus was talking over me.

"Folks. People. Enforcement is starting the wipe," he said in a flat voice. "They started it anyway. They started it anyway. They're killing Mennenkaltenei."

CHAPTER SIX

Maintaining Distance between Opponents (*Bumper Gap*, With Mismatch)

Nobody said anything for nearly a minute. It was so quiet I could hear the click of Cully's beads. Something rustled outside the window in the weedy garden.

"They wiped Mennenkaltenei in spite of us?" said Electra. Gray Julia looked even grayer than before.

Pegeen said, "Well, shall we have a chorus of 'but they can't do that!' and get it over with?"

"But they really *can't* do that," said Roder. "The petition should have stopped them. The NeverMind will shut them down completely."

Pegeen looked at him over her glasses. "Will it? Can it?"

"Be realistic. They might not need witches to run their engines, but they still need the NeverMind."

"That we know of," said Pegeen.

"Communication. Information storage and processing. News. They can't just sidestep the Web. The galaxy's too big, there's too much going on."

"So say they've made their own black-matter Web. Say they can communicate with the new stuff."

Roder sighed. "Oh, Pegeen, don't be paranoid."

"That's it," she insisted. "That's got to be it. That's why they've put so much work into developing the black-matter drive. It isn't just to reduce the dependence on witches, it's so they won't have to depend on the NeverMind itself."

Fergus nodded slowly, but Roder wasn't going to listen, though she was right. "We'd better find out what happened on Mennenkaltenei to make them do this." He leaned over the kidnapped

38

native and put something to his neck, then stood back, putting his hand on Octavian's arm. The communications officer's boyish face was tired and his skin had a damp shine to it, but when Roder touched him he seemed to settle in on himself and relax. Now I knew what Roder and his group reminded me of: a man I'd known on Fetuu who had seventeen dogs. When he took them for a walk, it was hard to tell who owned whom or who was in charge, except they expected a great deal more of him than he expected of them.

The Mennenkalt opened his eyes, clutched his staff, sat up, and twisted around to retrieve his hat as if he had known exactly where it was all along. He placed it firmly on his head, tugging the brim down all the way around. Then, using the staff, he stood up, with the crew of the ship taking a step back from him. He looked just as annoyed as he had before Roder knocked him out.

"Elder, your world has been destroyed by the Enforcers," said Roder. "I took the liberty of rescuing you."

"You were too hasty. I was permitted to stay behind because I had a vision and a mission," the Mennenkalt said. He peered up into Cully's face. He shook his head, and then walked over to Julia. She lowered her eyes. No, Julia wouldn't do either. I was afraid I knew what was coming. I went over to the window and looked out. The cat was washing one ragged ear out by the stone wall. It froze when it saw me.

"Mine," it said. It stared at me with blank gold eyes, and then gradually began to wash again. It had a patch of fur missing over one shoulder. If it were the familiar of a dead witch, it was going to lose more fur. It would turn into a rack of cat bones with a skin slung over it, and then into a small pile of something like fallen leaves. Then it would blow away. That was what happened most of the time.

Behind me everybody was talking at once, and then Roder's voice said, "Malka?"

He'd heard me say my name. I thought no one had noticed. I swung around. The native was pointing at me. Oh, well.

"Kurfurst lle zhatter," he said when he was sure he had my

attention. "Ekestverte yer andanfellter, kavelnes lle helster." I scowled. Mennenkalts.

Fergus said, "He wants to cure her constipation?" He really didn't speak Mennenkalt very well.

"The pronoun 'lle' makes a difference, Fergus," said Roder.

"I don't think she understands the language," said Electra helpfully.

I understood him fine. He was saying, "O, shackled spirit, consent to aid us and we will release you at the foreseen time," just like the Mennenkalts were always saying to me.

"No," I said. In Standard.

The native repeated to me very slowly and clearly, as if like Electra he thought I merely didn't understand, "Kurfurst lle zhatter, ekestverte yer andanfellter, kavelnes lle helster."

No. Go away, I said inside my head.

He bowed his head to me. "Kavelnes lle," he repeated once again, with great respect. He swept them all with a look and made a gesture with his hand.

"Oh, no, he disappeared," said Pegeen and they all put their hands out to try to catch him. Confused for a moment, not understanding that the others couldn't see him anymore, I watched him duck under Cully's arms and slip sideways out the half-open door.

Roder said, making me jump, "Malka, what is he doing?"

I pointed.

The crew rushed to the door and right past the Mennenkalt, who was standing with his back to the wall. "Hey," I said, but they didn't listen, and he was following them now anyway. He pushed a door open behind them and went in. "Hey!" I said again, and went to the door. It was the engine chamber, and he was standing in the middle looking completely normal. "Wow," I said. I'd never seen a human do that. The others shoved up around me and looked too, but of course they couldn't see anything.

Inside the engine, the Mennenkalt held his staff, with his chin up. He had his hat at his chest as if he were in church. His eyes were bright. "Lle kepelst, lle begest, lle koppelteren ne hals bekmelter," he said to the empty air, and then he began to fade from sight. He saw me and bowed again, then disappeared. Nice trick. Use somebody else's engine to squirt you through the Web.

"What are you looking at?" asked Roder, peering through his fingers at the empty engine room.

"Nothing, now. He went away." I closed the door again.

"Oh, damn," said Pegeen. "He deep-fried himself? Are you sure?" They started going back down the hall, but Roder stayed, looking down at me.

"He went away? Where did he go?" the android asked me politely. Cully glanced over his shoulder and slowed.

"He asked the engine to take him to his people."

"Oh, sweetie," said Electra, "you don't have to make anything up. It's all right."

"He said, 'Thou spirit be adored, thou spirit be respected, thou spirit take me to my people,' and he disappeared," I said to her, narrowing my eyes.

"Oh, for heaven's sake," said Electra, turning away. "What a show, child."

I narrowed my eyes some more, but she wasn't looking.

Roder looked amused. " 'To my people,' hm?"

"Ha." Pegeen stopped. "His people would normally be on Mennenkalt—"

"—but there aren't any Mennenkalts left on Mennenkaltenei, not if Enforcement did the wipe," Cully interrupted.

"Exactly," Roder agreed.

"Mennenkalts don't travel. They won't use magic that way," said Pegeen.

Roder said slowly, "I would have said they wouldn't use magic in *any* way that would upset Enforcement."

"You're saying they ran away before the wipe? Where?"

"We can find out, if it's a world in the Web," said Roder, and grinned at Octavian.

Octavian groaned. "Oh, my head. Come on, Roder. Please. There's more than a thousand worlds in the Web."

"Then we'd better get to work," said Roder. Pegeen rolled her eyes and slipped her arm around Octavian's waist. They all moved back to the kitchen down the hall.

"I need to talk to you," said Roder. "Come on."

I followed him. A talk about what? There were so many things I didn't want to talk about.

The third door down in the hall opened to his touch, though it had been locked when I tried it before, and he showed me in. It was a cold shadowy room, all smooth metal, and there were tall human-sized tanks in slots along one wall. In the fourth slot over was Tobiah.

He was naked in a blue-tinted fluid, his eyes closed and his hair waving in a slow current. I stopped and looked at him. Roder drew me to a stool in the far corner and sat me down facing him.

"First, I want to take care of some routine business. May I?" he said, holding his palms up facing me. He was asking if he could touch me.

I didn't move.

He put the hands back down on his legs. "Just a physical exam."

I didn't see what I could do to stop him, and he wasn't asking me to take my armor off. I nodded slowly.

With a blank face, he quickly, lightly ran his hands down the tops of my arms and up the undersides, down the rib cage to my hips, then repeated the sweep with my legs, as if he were feeling my skin through the armor.

"Stand up and face away from me." I could feel the travel of his hands down my back, up the back of my neck. It was as impersonal as falling rain. He felt behind my ears and slid his fingers over my cap. Then he had me sit down again so he could trace the orbits of my eyes, press down either side of my nose, and look up my nostrils. Even when his hands were directly on my skin, he did it without the meaning that humans always gave to touch.

"Hm. Open your mouth."

I didn't. I shook my head.

After waiting a beat, he leaned back against the counter. "It's all right. I would just like to measure your temperature. That's why I asked."

"Everything in the universe has a temperature," I said, keeping my mouth narrow. I didn't let people take my temperature since that doctor on Halyard got so upset, and it hadn't gone down any since then.

The mournful river-colored eyes rested on me. He took a breath to say something and thought better of it.

"All right. Let's have our talk. What would you like to know about us?" he said.

It was the one thing I hadn't expected. What would I like to know? I tried to think of something to ask him that wouldn't give me away.

So I pointed at Tobiah.

"Him? I am mending him." He walked over and regarded Tobiah, who looked as if he had drowned while asleep, though now I could see the slow ripple of his ribs as he breathed something, not air, in and out. "Enforcement delivers my recruits in poor condition. They tell me he's a chronologer, but he's got some stuff inside him I can't identify, and he doesn't read as a witch on my scans."

I nodded. Silence.

"What else can I tell you?"

I thought. "What are you?"

"What am I or what do I do? You knew *what* I was when you saw my face."

That almost stopped me, but I said, "I mean what do you do."

"I'm a Monitor. I work for the government. I monitor Enforcement. I'm a glorified referee with a little shiny whistle. I blow it whenever Enforcement goes over the boundaries."

I didn't laugh. That made sense. I'd always thought the Monitors were nothing but a fairy tale, but apparently they actually existed. Once upon a time, the government had a dim clue it wasn't a good idea to create a police force that had unlimited power, so they created a mosquito, gave it perfect freedom, and sent it to buzz about Enforcement's ears . . . Tobiah had turned a quarter inch to the right while Roder was talking, not a voluntary movement but a combination of breathing and flow inside his container.

"So you already know about Monitors, too," said the android, startling me. He leaned against the tank.

"Are you going to put me in one of those now?" I pointed to the tank.

"No. You don't have any suspicious implants and you're not injured, so no, I won't put you in there. I don't use the stasis tanks for cages. This is an infirmary, not a jail."

I set my jaw. He could try that on somebody else.

"You're not the first recruit to try to kill me, Malka," he said. "Pegeen used a knife."

"I bet I—" I stopped.

"No. She wasn't nearly as good as you are. She didn't even come close. Mostly they try to use magic on me instead, but I'm completely encased in shielding. In case you were wondering."

I shifted around uncomfortably.

"I need a crew. I can't drive an engine or do a proper investigation without witches. But I can't use the Polytechnic graduates. They're conditioned too well. They'd have nervous breakdowns trying to even think about Enforcement the way my crew needs to. So under the law, Enforcement supplies me with unconditioned witches right out of their nets, whenever I ask. Some of my recruits try to kill me, like you. Some of them aren't in such good shape, like this gentleman. I'm used to it."

I didn't say anything. It sounded like a bad deal all around, for everybody concerned.

"We're in here now because I have some standard hiring procedures. I'm going to make sure you're healthy, give you an implant so I can ID you to Enforcement when you're off the ship, and socket you in to officially record your hiring."

I shook my head.

His face went blank. Inconvenient Malka. "Why not?"

"Doesn't work," I said, showing him the socket in my right palm.

A long pause, while he stared at it. "A forgery. It must have been hard to get that done, but why? It just gives ID?"

I nodded. That was all it did. It wasn't a line to my brain, it was a local echo that went no farther than my wrist.

"Do you want a real one you can use? I can give you one."

"Won't take," I said.

"Won't take? Your brain rejects it? So I guess I can't give you a locator implant either?"

I shrugged and repeated, "Won't take."

He sat back on the counter and swung his legs. I watched Tobiah breathe blue fluid.

"So. Tell me about yourself," he said.

I could feel my jaw muscles ache. *No.* Nothing to tell.

"No? Then I'll tell you about yourself." He held up his fingers and folded them down one by one as he talked. "You tell me you're not a witch. You don't have a familiar that I can find. But your shielding is better than mine—I couldn't detect any body functions just now. You can walk in and out of an active engine, see what's inside, and see people when they're invisible. You speak Mennenkalt, and probably Matrish—you understand Fergus when he swears. You're an expert Caliban sword-fighter, but you're not a Caliban. You figured out the homeworld of every one of my crew in less than a minute. I watched you do it."

It was just as impersonal as his hands, and just as steady. *No. Stop it.* It was louder than I'd intended.

Roder swung his legs again, looking vague, and then gathered himself with a visible effort.

"Corrections? No? I'll go on. The forged palm socket you have was made for a very short time thirty years ago, on Didrika. You looked at my face and knew I was an android. The company hasn't made a new Massim in over sixty years, and there weren't that many of us to begin with."

I began to see where he was going, and pushed my heels down as if braking a slide downhill.

"And you're Forest born and bred. I'd swear to it. But Forest was wiped forty years ago, and I was there to see it. So even though Electra seems sure you're about fifteen, you're—what?"

I scrambled off the stool and drew my sword, backing away from him, but he didn't stop swinging his legs. He didn't look pleased with himself, though.

"Fifty? Fifty-five? And you've managed to avoid Enforcement for half a century?"

I crouched, ready to defend myself.

He stilled his legs. We stared at each other. He was taking me seriously, just as he did when I attacked him before, but he wasn't backing down, either.

Once again, we passed some critical moment, and he relaxed. "I'm sorry I upset you. I'll ask you how you did it some other time. You can come back in when you're ready."

He left the room, closing the door, and left me crouched over, all my muscles tense.

I screamed at the top of my voice, and jumped up and down. I whirled in place, swinging the sword so it hissed. Then I did it again. Then I climbed back onto the stool and sat there with my eyes closed, breathing in and out, holding the sides of the stool. It was like somebody had taken my skin off whole and then handed it back to me so I could put it back on, and it was the handing back part that bothered me . . . The skin where I had hit Zul was red, right between the grimy edge of his collar and the roots of his beard, and I dropped my weapon and said I was sorry. I said I was sorry. And I had not killed Roder, or Cully.

I must be falling apart at the seams. It was inevitable. I wasn't meant to get this big.

There was a scratching noise at the door. I opened my eyes, and for a moment it looked as if Tobiah were staring at me in fury from his blue tank, but then something scratched at the door again. I got up and opened the door, looking out and then down. It was the gray cat, its tail wrapped around it. "Mine. Mine," it said, lifting its crumpled whiskers with each syllable.

"Yes. Yours," I said. "I'm just passing through. I'm leaving as soon as I can." It walked in anyway, waited until I sat down again, and then jumped up into my lap with its back against me, its shabby sides pumping in and out with a silent purr. The cat smelled ugly, not ugly like the Sefir Zul but ugly like old butter. With each breath it sent tufts of fur above it in the air, where they hung like smoke and disappeared. The cat was falling apart at the seams too, poor thing. I put my hand down on it, and it laid its chin on my hand and closed its eyes. I watched it for a while. Fifty-five years ago, my master's dog Bear liked me, better than he liked my master, but I couldn't remember now what Bear even looked like.

CHAPTER SEVEN

The Probing Attack (*Arachne's Needle,* For Finding Out)

When I got uncomfortable, I tried to put the cat down on the floor carefully, but it started struggling and ended up jumping down with a thud and darting out the door. When I looked out, the hall seemed dimmer than ever, though there was a gap of light beneath the kitchen door. It was some kind of official night on the ship. In the kitchen, it was dark outside that window too, but the crew of the ship was busy and no one looked up when I came in.

Octavian, slim and supple, lay on the floor with his chin on his hands. His eyes were closed but you could see them flicker under his eyelids as he said, "No . . . No . . . No . . ." while Electra read him a list of planet names. Pegeen sat on a chair next to him, with her feet together and her dark hands over her bespectacled eyes, nodding when he spoke. Wladyslaw was staring at a screen scrolling data so fast it blurred, somebody's backup text records.

Roder, like the rest, was watching Octavian, but I was sure he saw me come in, though he didn't look right away. He shifted his eyes to look at me, just slowly enough that I could be looking away myself before our eyes met. Not only did he see things, he knew when he shouldn't see things. He said, "We're trying to find the Mennenkalts."

I still didn't look at him. He continued, "There wasn't anybody left on the planet when it was wiped. The Mennenkalts all left before it happened."

He was still looking at me. I could feel it on the side of my face. I didn't know where they'd gone. Just because Mennenkalts recognized me when they saw me didn't mean I understood them.

He finally said, "Whatever they did or didn't do to deserve the wipe, they're in for it now. Flight to avoid discipline is a Class One offense."

"I guess that blows their religious exemption," said Fergus.

I'd never quite understood how the Mennenkalts pulled off the exemption as long as they had, though it might just have been a grandfather clause in the Control Act. They'd been around forever. They believed magic was god, they ate their kings, and they were stuffy and boring and obsessed with food, crops, and fertility. They took immigrants, though they turned down the ones who were interested in them for their sexual practices. I had tried to emigrate there once, but they told me I was a benighted slave and they attempted to free me from my spiritual bondage, right then and there in the immigration office.

"Gagarin . . . Annawon . . . Tatanka Iyota . . . Worthy Montgomery . . . ," said Electra in the silence.

"No . . . No . . . No . . . No . . . ," answered Octavian to each one.

Cully slid his beads through his fingers. "It doesn't make sense. They're so conservative. So rigid and moralistic. It would take something outrageous for them to defy Enforcement."

"Um," I said, and again nobody heard me but Roder.

"Yes?" he said.

"Enforcement disciplined Mennenkalt three years ago," I said. It was a planet-wide punishment, the one for a Class Three offense. Enforcement executed all the government officials above department head, deported random chunks of the population, dumped refugees on Mennenkaltenei, and poisoned the crops. It happened just after I tried to emigrate.

"I would have heard about it," he said, and I supposed that was that.

"Monahan . . . Polydionysus . . . Chapman . . . Laelah's Mask . . . ," read Electra.

"No . . . No . . . No . . . No . . ."

"Enforcement just didn't happen to get around to notifying

you this time either, Roder," said Pegeen, with her hands still over her eyes.

"You're really being paranoid now, Pegeen," said Electra, interrupting herself.

Roder opened his mouth, and closed it again, then looked at me. I shrugged, but he kept waiting.

"It was a Class Three offense," I said. "Breeding for the gift."

"They're allowed to encourage the birth of witches, sweetheart," explained Electra. "It's part of their religion." I wished I hadn't said anything.

Roder said, "Where did they put the people they deported? They usually dump them on the next planet they punish."

I shrugged. *Leave me alone,* I thought.

Roder seemed lost in thought. Cully, who had been hunched over his station, swiveled around in his chair and watched us, fingering his beads.

Electra continued, "Gitalong 2 . . . Morbid . . . Eight Horses . . . Ong's Hat . . . Guilty as Charged . . ."

"No . . . No . . . No . . . No . . . No . . ."

"How do you do that?" Cully asked me suddenly, and Roder glanced at him under his brows.

"How does she do what?"

"She did it before. She mutters under her breath, and people do what she says."

"No, I don't."

"Roder asked you a question, you said, 'Leave me alone,' and all of a sudden he didn't care anymore."

"I did not. I didn't say anything."

Roder laughed. "So that's what— When we were talking a little while ago, in the infirmary, it felt like someone was hitting me with a hammer. Malka, you're a witch, all right. You're not only an immune, you're a spell speaker. No, you didn't say anything, but you're so strong you don't have to open your mouth."

I set my mouth grimly, and flinched when they all laughed.

"Speaker," said Wladyslaw, his eyes not leaving the screen. "Talks about as much as mud."

"Just *leave me alone,*" I said, aloud this time.

Pegeen took her hands off her eyes momentarily. "I see what you mean, Cully. That made my head ache. So *can* we leave her alone now? We need to finish this."

Roder nodded.

"And so you get what you wish," said Cully. "No, no, don't say it," holding up his hands to stop me.

I went to the window. It was dark outside, and I couldn't make out the fishpond or the stone walls, just a darker blur below the horizon and a deep gray sky above, a different sky than the one outside my bedroom. This moth-eaten little houseboat must have a different space-fold outside every window. The cat jumped up to the windowsill next to me and leaned on me, hard, ramming the top of its head into my arm.

"Heaven . . . Carmichael . . ."

"No . . . No . . ."

Wladyslaw, still staring at the scrolling screen, froze it suddenly and said, "Here it is. Three and a half years ago. Class Three offense. Genetic manipulation contrary to Title Eight of the Control Act. Twelve thousand Mennenkalts were loaded on the *Hilma K. Lewis*, and they're still on board."

"Still on the ship?" said Fergus in horror. "Brother Conrad's tail-wrap. Sorry. But really."

Knowing the Mennenkalts, Enforcement was saving them to dump on some planet that really ticked them off.

"Where's the *Hilma K.* now?" asked Roder, ignoring Fergus.

Wladyslaw answered doubtfully, "At backup time, it was off the Web chasing a prisoner that got away."

The whole group laughed. "One of those Mennenkalt farmers saw a cow that needed milking outside, and there was no stopping him," said Fergus.

"Victoria . . ." said Electra firmly, bringing them back to task.

"No," answered Octavian, still chuckling.

"Caliban 5 . . ."

There was a long delay. At last, Octavian said, "No answer. Can't get through to their Cybernal. The Forcers have it locked for administrative review."

"But we were just there! Oh well, we'll come back to it. Hovering Flower . . ." Electra sounded annoyed.

"No . . ." They continued.

Administrative review. My sharp-nosed thin-lipped master was getting swifter. He'd already been in and out of Caliban looking for me, and they were all busy locking the stable doors now. I needed to get off this ship before he tracked it down. My little persistent master. I could feel the hairs on the backs of my arms standing up.

"Octavian's querying every planet Mind to find out if they've logged any Mennenkalt visitors," explained Cully next to my elbow, running a finger down the cat's back so that it arched happily. I turned my face away slightly. I didn't want to be friends with him, I wanted to be friends with the cat, and he was being condescending. I knew very well what Octavian was doing.

"Dobrovolski . . ."

"No . . ."

"Nitoh Mahkwi . . . Lazarus . . . ," read Electra.

"No . . . Yes," said Octavian, opening his eyes. "Yes, yes, yes. Lazarus. Mennenkalt agents bought all the old-style gray-matter ships in the Somnus Terminal yards, paid cash, supplied the crews, and left over the course of a week."

"Lazarus it is, then," said Roder. "Fergus?"

Fergus plugged in, and grimaced. "Woof, the engine's in a bad mood. Lazarus, Lazarus," and his face went still as he spoke to the magic furnace back in that empty room. "Ahh . . . okay," he finally said. "Prepare for translation."

They all went pale. Being in translation never bothered me. Humans said being neither-here-nor-there was some kind of a transcendent state. The idea was, when they were in translation they were inside the nonlocal universe of magic where all places were one place, all times one time, and all things were one thing. They could think thoughts, understand ideas, imagine things they never would let pass through their minds otherwise. From the way it looked, they weren't very agreeable thoughts.

Pegeen, for instance, looked as if she were repressing a belch, and gray Julia looked even grayer. Cully had his eyes closed and his head rolling back as if he were trying to unkink a stiff neck. "This is our fourth translation today," complained Octavian in a faint voice, shifting around, and nobody bothered to respond. They were all linked in their uneasy discomfort. Roder was watching me again, so maybe his expression had to do with another thing he'd noticed about me. I hoped not.

The cat was washing one paw complacently. She didn't feel it either.

It was a short translation. My stomach jumped as the ship tilted sideways, the crew looked relieved, and then the floor thumped and the ship gave a settling lurch. "Somnus," said Fergus on a descending note, looking truculent.

"Right. We'll talk about that landing later," said Roder. "Electra, you and I go to the terminal offices to interview the station-master. Julia, tap the data stream from the station to the Lazarus Cybernal and see if you can find flight plans for the Mennen-kalts. Pegeen, conceal Wladyslaw so he can get into the transaction record backups; I don't have time to go through official channels to request them. Fergus, Octavian, check the gossip in the crew lounge and *please* don't make any unnecessary comments about the Polytechnic. Cully . . ." He raised his eyebrows at the tall Calypsan and nodded at me.

"Baby-sit," finished the priest, nodding. The room emptied except for Roder, Cully, and me. Cully stretched his long legs out and began sliding his beads along their cord very slowly with both hands, concentrating on the task. There was still a spot of blood on the front of his tunic. He hadn't bothered to change it.

Roder, still sitting, said to me, "I advise you not to leave the ship, but it's up to you."

I didn't move. Didn't say anything.

"Cully's not your guard. He's here to keep you company and keep anybody from getting into the ship while we're away. Cully, you aren't to try to restrain her in any way, understand?"

Cully said, with emphasis, "No problem."

"Malka?" said Roder.

I waited for him to leave.

"You remember Electra mentioned Akamai, the woman who died? She went outside on Rilievo when I asked her not to go, and without notifying the Rilievo Cybernal. As a member of my crew, she wasn't a wild witch anymore. She was a deserter, and therefore Enforcement treated her differently than they would a wild witch. They didn't try to catch her. They just killed her."

Enforcement wasn't the problem, if I could sneak aboard another ship fast enough. My nasty little master was the problem. He could make me do whatever he wanted.

Roder exchanged a look with Cully, and left. Cully slid another bead, and didn't look at me.

Out in the hall, doors were banging and there were footsteps and voices. I looked, and they were all wearing armbands that reflected the light as they trooped out. I glanced at Cully, and he still wasn't looking at me.

I waited about a minute, walked down the hall, opened the door, and looked out. It was day here, though it was night on the ship. We were in another terminal like Eliot, though it wasn't in the center of a city. Here the air smelled of clay, damp, and moss. There were fewer ships, and the sky had a yellow tinge to it like the inside of a melon. The crew members were going down the alley between the lines of parked ships.

I stepped out. The surface was a deep gray ceramic, and beyond the rows of ships I couldn't see any fence, just a marshy expanse of grass and some low buildings at a distance. I couldn't remember anything about Lazarus, though I'd been here once. It was hot, and my armor felt like a turtle shell. I went to the edge. The grassy marsh sucked at me when I tried to put a foot down in it, so I went down the alley where the crew had gone.

When I had gone no more than ten feet, a bulbous orange shape winked into the sky, a small Enforcement patrol ship, and it dropped and squatted down in an empty parking spot between two ships just ahead of me. A front hatch slid up and two orange figures stood framed against the interior, their arms folded, looking in the direction the crew had gone. I stopped. *No.*

Then another orange ship came down across from them, and another. The third one was a full-size transport that lowered its hold door and began unloading orange-and-gray vans. The two Forcers in the first ship turned their heads. They jumped down and ran toward me. I drew my sword with a hiss.

Then two more Forcers appeared in the hatchway, and I turned and ran.

I ran back to Roder's ship, but the front door had closed and locked behind me. I hammered with my fist once, then again. *No.* I could hear their footsteps.

Cully swung the door in and walked away as I jumped back in.

I carefully closed the door and stood just inside, breathing in the air of the old ship. No noise came from outside. I ran my finger along the plaster wall, feeling the damp, the cracks, and the holes in it as I walked back to the kitchen. The floor creaked under me.

Cully moved a bead along the loose cord, then moved it back. "How many Enforcement ships?" he asked.

"Three."

He sighed, and met my eyes, then shifted them away.

"Do they . . . ," I began, then stopped.

"Do they follow us everywhere? Yes. Can they do that? Yes. As long as they don't interfere with our work. Can they kill us? Yes. If we leave without permission, or if they can make it look like a mistake."

A soggy night breeze blew across the garden outside the kitchen window, ruffling the ferns and rippling the surface of the fishpond.

"You might as well resign yourself to it. Settle down, settle in. This is your home now."

Home? I didn't think so. It was a mobile prison. It was a leghold trap, meant for some other kind of animal, but its jaws had closed on me instead. I was trapped here until my master came to punish me. I had better start getting ready.

CHAPTER EIGHT

The Footwork Pattern (*Astaire*, With Known Opponent)

When the door slammed open, I had been practicing for an hour, and still had an hour to go. Two hours of footwork a day, no matter what, the Sefir Zul said.

The foot is the most important part of sword-fighting, not the hand. Beginners don't know that. If you hand a beginner a blade, he plants his feet and waves the blade around, or thrusts with it, or chops. That's because he doesn't understand that the blow is only the finish of a sword-fight, not the beginning. In order to end the fight, you have to move. You need to be too far away for your opponent to hit you, and close enough for you to hit him, and you need to convince your opponent that he's close enough to hit you and too far away to get hit. That sounds like a joke, but it's not.

I watched the Sefir Zul demonstrate this to a novice, a few weeks after I got over the humiliation of having it done to me. Zul dropped his weapon, and the novice charged forward to attack, raising his blade high. Zul retreated smoothly, then halted his retreat an instant, like a hiccup, before continuing backward one more step, an elementary Radomil maneuver. Fooled by Zul's tiny pause, the beginner swung his blade too early, missed him, and nearly fell over with the force of his swing. Zul smacked him on the top of the head with his blade and sneered.

Bewildered, the man took up his on-guard position again, and this time he decided to wait for Zul's attack. Zul stepped forward, bringing his shining weapon up in a sharp motion before he was really within striking distance, the straight Taylor feint. The novice jerked his blade across to parry the false threat, missed Zul's weapon entirely, and stood in dismay as

56

Zul stood with his blade bent in an arc, point buried in the student's cotton armor.

"You're just too fast for me," said the novice, trying to laugh.

"Not too fast, too far," said Zul and slapped him on the side of the head so the man glared with his jaw thrust out, obviously not understanding. I don't remember the beginner's name. He didn't come back for his second class.

I hated Zul too, and not just because he probably washed his face with his tongue and farmed mushrooms in his armpits. He made no secret of his contempt and impatience for me. "Troll girl," he called me. "Time for the troll's lesson. Come, troll," and I would march over and stand grimly on guard while the other students laughed. I never understood why he insisted on keeping me as a student.

He smelled bad, he was unkind to me, and he didn't care if I lived or died, but the lessons were a dance of understanding for me. From the first grudging salute to the last, they were a conversation conducted at sword's length, without words, and even if they always ended with Zul smacking me, I learned something new every time.

Even though he showed me no favor, the other students resented me. They didn't think anyone but a Caliban should study in a Caliban school. They made fun of my size and my temper. When we free-fought, they went for the painful spots, and they struck with too much force. For the first year I hurt all over. Then, when I finally learned to use my feet, they stopped being able to hit me.

So now I made each movement perfect. I concentrated on form, practiced each foot action separately, and then combined them into patterns. I tried not to think about where I was, though the smell of the air kept intruding. The ship was almost as old as I was, and so was Roder, but both of them were expensive when they were new. How long had he been buzzing around the ears of Enforcement without getting swatted? Longer than I had, though he could do it out in the open.

No, I wouldn't be distracted. I would practice my footwork. My skin was sweating, my feet were burning, my legs were aching. I wouldn't think of myself as a captive. I might be imprisoned for the moment, but I was a mighty sword-fighter and I would fight my way out of this. I was the Prisoner Malka, scraping away at her shackles with a pebble, keeping her skills strong, laboring in the dead of night while the Forces of Evil ran ceaselessly outside, barking.

That was when the front door crashed open. The Prisoner Malka squeaked in surprise and flattened against the wall, her heart pounding.

Roder charged past me carrying Pegeen in his arms. He was followed by Electra, her face swollen and dark stains down the front of her clothes. Roder disappeared into the infirmary. Octavian and Fergus tore through the door a moment later, and Fergus slammed it shut behind him. He stopped halfway down the corridor to lean on his thighs and gasp. Octavian grabbed him by the upper arm and pulled him along. "I have to breathe," Fergus protested.

"Later," Octavian said. "Breathe later." He sounded as if he'd been crying. He pulled Fergus into the kitchen.

I looked into the open door of the infirmary. Roder was leaning on his arms against the third stasis tank, where dark brown Pegeen floated in the middle of a cloud of darker liquid that was draining out of her.

In the fourth tank, Tobiah Gregg lifted his chin, shook his head slowly, and closed his eyes again.

While I was frozen staring at him, Roder stood up. I quickly got out of the doorway and Roder slid past me and into the kitchen. I heard Fergus say, in response to something Roder had said, "I'm working on it, I'm working on it!"

There was a thud. It came from the direction of the front door. Roder came out and pushed past me again. Another thud came, more like a boom this time. Roder put his hands to the door, moving them about as if he were blind. The next thud made his fingers vibrate, but he kept them pressed against the panel.

Boom. The inside of the door bulged this time, and he backed away. "Fergus!" he said.

"Keep your bottom on," yelled Fergus.

Octavian stuck his head out. "Engine trouble, boss."

"We can't afford engine trouble," Roder said calmly. "They're using a shock cannon." Boom. The door bulged again and subsided, though this time it wasn't quite flat when the force of the impact went away.

"Right. No engine trouble." Octavian popped back into the kitchen.

I looked down and saw my sword still in my hand, my knuckles white and the grip all wrong. I was holding it like a club. It didn't matter. My little pointy stick wouldn't stop whatever was hitting the door.

The next boom finished with a high screech. The peak of the bulge had a white crown of frayed door, as if something sharp had almost penetrated. The door snapped back again, but now there was a protruding dimple. Roder took another step back, stood with his legs apart, and put his arms behind his back as if he were standing at attention.

In the pause between that shock and the next, there was absolute silence. Then came another boom, and a tearing sound, and then a crunch so loud it made me lean with the impact. The door ruptured, sending sparkling splinters bouncing down the hall in a corona around the android. One came to rest by my foot, a translucent glass shard that looked like the door surface on only one side. Roder brushed his face off and I heard more splinters falling from him. Through the torn opening in the door there was bright daylight and movement, and then something dark swung forward, blotted out the light, and struck the door once again, distending the hole and rolling its edges back. When the dark bludgeon swung back, and let the light back in, Roder still didn't move.

A large head appeared in the aperture. Against the bright light, all I could see was thick stiff hair standing on end, and then it disappeared and a big orange-covered arm was reaching through the hole, groping for the doorknob. He couldn't reach.

"You are out of your jurisdiction," said Roder. "I am going to file an official protest."

That was it? That was how he planned to defend us? I took a step forward.

The man withdrew his arm.

"Fergus, *please,*" called Roder, almost quietly.

The battering ram slammed against the door again, and widened the hole. After it swung back, the man appeared again, groping blindly but with complete scorn for whoever might be watching. This time the hand almost reached the doorknob.

"This ship and its employees are the property of the Department of Monitoring and Compliance, and not to be tampered with," said Roder in a conversational tone. I was right behind him now.

The hand pulled out again. This time the tip of the conical ram nearly touched Roder's face when it swung through, tearing the hole to shoulder width. The android didn't flinch.

"You have to kill him," I said. "You have to fight back."

"I can't," he said calmly. "I wish I could. I have my limits. I can run, I can hide, I can argue, or I can file a protest, and if they kill me outright I have a transmitter implant that notifies the NeverMind. I can't use force against them."

"Can I?"

He thought about it.

The Enforcer's head thrust through again, and this time, because enough light surrounded it, I could see his face. I recognized it.

He peered down and checked the location of the doorknob. "You're fired," he said to Roder. I recognized his voice, too. He pulled his head out, stuck his arm in, seized the doorknob—

—and, raising my arm as if I were holding a butcher knife and not a precision instrument, I ducked under Roder's arm and nailed the Enforcer's hand to the door, striking the Sefir Zul for the second time that day and drawing blood this time.

There was a familiar yell of rage. I yanked the point of my sword out, and the arm whipped away. Zul's head appeared again, looking, and I poked at it like a woodpecker, but the head slipped aside. Roder slid out of my way and put his back to the wall, watching me.

"Troll," said Zul's voice contemptuously from the other side of the door. "You think you are my student. I taught you nothing. Nothing. Nothing."

I listened.

"You hack at me from behind a wall, like a frightened animal. Fight me as a fighter should, face-to-face. Come out and fight me."

I shifted my grip on the sword.

"You are afraid? You are afraid? The Sefir Malka with all her fancy armor is afraid of a mere Zul? You struck me twice today—can you not do it again?" he taunted, his voice thick.

I bent my knees, and breathed hard. He never talked this much. I knew what he was trying to do. I struggled to keep him from getting me to do it.

There were other voices outside, arguing. "Be silent," Zul snapped. Now there were muttered complaints. In a harsh whisper, deliberately loud enough for me to hear, Zul said, "I trained her. I know her. She has the bad temper of a squirrel monkey, and less brains."

He stuck his face back in the hole. I stabbed at it again, and missed again, and he laughed. "Come out and get me, Malka," he said. "Or kill the android for me, like you were supposed to. You weren't good enough, were you?"

I reached for the doorknob, and Roder's fingers were grasping my wrist, lightly. "Don't touch me," I hissed, white-hot, glaring at him. He separated his fingers gently. He was still leaning against the wall, watching me with that grave expression. We stared at each other.

An arm, holding a needle-gun, came through the hole next to my head and shot down the corridor, once, twice, three times. I could hear the spitting sound of the needles hitting the kitchen door.

I still couldn't move. *Help,* I said in my head. *Help.* Malka the Paralyzed in Battle. Roder flinched and closed his eyes.

I raised my blade, saw something, and stuck there, frozen in place. The arm was wearing orange, but it wasn't big enough to be Zul's. He'd sent a sacrifice in his place.

Go. Leave now, I said shakily. *LEAVE.*

There was a cheer from the kitchen.

I still held my blade high, but all by itself the arm fell to the floor, the hand falling open and the gun falling from its fingers.

Through the hole in the door I could see Nothing. We were in translation, and the Forcer's arm was the only part of him that got to make the trip with us.

CHAPTER NINE

The Establishment of Tempo (*Marching Band,* Taking Control)

I stood with the sword in my hand. The tip was red. The Sefir Zul taught me never to put a sword back in the scabbard bloody. But then, the Sefir Zul was an Enforcer, and everything he told me was a lie. I leaned against the wall opposite Roder.

"Three years," I said. "I was with him for three years."

I could hear him breathing. "Are you all right?" he said finally.

Well, no, I was not all right. Now that I had reason to distrust the Sefir Zul, I didn't believe anything he did. He had given up too easily just now. It smelled, just like the scene with the Forcer in Zul's academy this morning would have smelled if I'd used my common sense. It was like the inlay in Tobiah's clock, one set of layers concealing another set.

I heard Roder's feet moving away, and then the kitchen door closed.

My scalp was burning. Absently, I rubbed it and said, "Ooh," staring at my wet hand. The Forcer shooting down the hall had been aiming for my head, not the kitchen door. The tip of the dart had missed, but it scraped my scalp on the way past.

Three years. The Sefir Zul took me on because he thought I had potential, not as a sword-fighter but as an ignorant assassin. A tool. A trained animal, a walking bomb, a rabid mole wrapped up as a present. I knew Enforcement had chased me directly to Roder, and now I knew why they had done it that way. They wanted him to believe they had nothing to do with my arrival, so he wouldn't mistrust me like poor Tobiah, wouldn't stick me in the stasis tank right away.

I hadn't killed Roder yet. I probably wouldn't kill him, either. But it still wasn't enough. The Sefir Zul always nested his real attacks within false attacks. I would have to be on guard. I would have to keep my eyes open. Something else would happen, I didn't know what or where or when.

The arm still lay on the floor, the needler next to it. I pitied the Enforcer who offered it up to me, now standing on Lazarus looking at his empty shoulder in shock while the Sefir Zul doubtless strode away, ignoring him.

I put the needler in my pocket, picked the arm up by the sleeve, and shoved it through the hole in the door, giving it a sharp push so it wouldn't just hang there. As the arm slid into Nothing, it ceased to exist. The information about the arm slipped the engine's mind completely. Conservation of energy and matter didn't exactly work in translation. After staring out the hole for a while, briefly homesick, I walked down the hall trailing my sword behind me with the tip on the floor. I didn't care for this game at all.

When I walked in, Fergus was glowering at the console and Electra was sitting at the table with an ice pack on her jaw. They all looked pale again. Nobody looked at me.

The room seemed to rise in the air and then fall, and I stumbled.

"*What* was that landing?" said Roder.

"I can't help it. I can't help it," said Fergus, yanking his palm off the socket. "The engine is ignoring me."

"Well, we're here, anyway. Octavian, put in a call to the Never-Mind." Octavian put his head in his hands and began jiggling and jittering again. He was sweating, and droplets flew off him as he shook. It seemed as if everybody in the room except Roder was vibrating with him, wavering in and out of view. I shook my head. *Concentrate,* I said.

"Ow!" said Octavian, sitting bolt upright and glaring at me.

"NeverMind!" Roder leaned forward.

"NeverNeverNever—" started Octavian in that rough voice, and began to cough.

"Code Monitor Roder Massim filing complaint against the Office of Enforcement, Regulation, and Control, alleging harassment and assault of employees of the Code Monitor, systematic hindrance of Code Monitor investigations in progress—"

"Enforcement ships landing," said Fergus.

Roder jerked around. "Already? How many ships?"

"Three, four . . . no, six now."

"Okay, take us out the moment Octavian's off-line. Try Cloud Farm. Nimbus City terminal, it's so big it'll take them half an hour to process us." He swung back to Octavian. "Where was I? Trespass on property of Code Monitor. That's it, I think. NeverMind?"

There was no answer. Octavian's mouth was open as if he were about to speak, but nothing came out. I noticed his makeup was smeared.

"NeverMind?" repeated Roder. "Don't lose the connection, Octavian. Stay in for the acknowledgment. Stay in."

"It's fading," said Octavian in a bewildered voice.

We were all leaning forward, as if we could shove him into closer contact with the NeverMind. *Focus, focus,* I realized I was saying inside my head.

"Ow!" he said again. "Complaint registered. NeverMind. Malka, don't do that."

"Okay, ready? Translation," snapped Fergus, and everybody looked even more ill than they had before, but relieved at the same time. The cat jumped up into the window and stretched luxuriously.

Still standing in the doorway, I looked around. The crew was all sitting with their hands dangling between their knees, looking shocked. No, not the whole crew. Where were gray Julia and the toothy, shy Wladyslaw?

"What happened out there?" said Cully. I braced myself.

Roder shook his head, but he didn't mention what had just happened in the hall. "Electra and I were talking to the stationmaster when Pegeen called for help. They had just started looking at the backup when Enforcement came in the building already shooting. Julia's signal stopped at the same time. Electra, Pegeen, and I were cut off from the yard, so we went outside, stole a taxi, and rammed the yard gates."

Electra said through the bag of ice. "I feel like I rammed them with my face. You could have told me we were going to do that."

"I'm sorry," Roder said, and he meant it, but she just closed her eyes.

Cully clutched his beads. "They just attacked? They didn't say anything?"

Roder shook his head. "Octavian, Fergus?"

"We hadn't even gotten to the driver's lounge," said Fergus. "There was a ruckus in the station so we turned around and ran. That's what we were doing when we met up with you."

"Pegeen was shot as we were coming up to the ship. They were still shooting as we were heading for our ship," said the android. He shook his head and kept shaking it.

"Is she all right?" Octavian burst out.

"What?" Roder looked up. "Pegeen? It's a shallow wound. She'll be fine."

"Still think she was being paranoid?" said Octavian.

"No. No. It's some kind of coup. I have to figure out some way that I can make myself think about this. I'm not designed for it." He looked down again, his face patient and tired. They all watched him expectantly, his pack of faithful, needy dogs.

Leave him alone, I said, and Cully said, "Protecting somebody else for a change, mouse?" Now they all looked at me.

I was not a mouse. I was Malka the Eternally Deluded, but I wasn't going to have people calling me a mouse.

"Hey. You're bloody," said Roder, leaning forward. "What happened to your head?" I put my hand up and felt it. The sharp pain had changed to a throbbing burn. "Did he shoot you?" He stopped running his hands over my scalp just before I was ready to hit him. "Come on. Infirmary for you."

"Well, I like that," said Electra fiercely through her ice bag. I didn't know if Roder heard her, because he left without commenting.

In the infirmary, the fluid around Pegeen was clear now, though there was a long ugly ditch across her belly. Her face was hard and still, and she was still wearing her glasses. One earpiece dangled free, bobbing. Roder sat me down and reached into a cabinet while I watched Tobiah. He'd always seemed young, but right now he looked like an unborn baby. I could see the pulse in his neck. His bones stuck out like a wet bird's and he was corpse-color.

"Don't look so nervous," said Roder. "I said you weren't the first of my crew to attack me. You're not even the first one planted on me. I find their efforts intriguing."

"I didn't know I was a plant. Well, I knew that Enforcement chased me here on purpose, but I didn't know he was behind it. That man was my sword-master. I thought he let me into the academy because I might be good."

"Calibans don't share," he said. I knew that. I should have known that.

"Ouch!" Roder had done something to my head that made it burn again, worse.

"I have to clean it. You lost more than scalp," continued Roder, reaching in the cabinet again. Tobiah's pulse seemed quick, fluttering rapidly like a small animal's, and he opened his eyes, blinked them, and shut them again. Roder began doing something that hurt even more. I concentrated on my breathing. "Good," said the android, swinging me around on the stool to face him. "Now. That will repair itself, but if you let me put you in the stasis tank for a little while, it will work faster and hurt less."

I shook my head.

"If you're afraid of being trapped, it's easy enough to set the controls so you can let yourself out."

I shook my head even more forcefully, and he smiled. "You're a tough character."

Malka the Tough. Malka the Leathery. Malka the Extremely Chewy. "Can he let himself out?" I pointed to Tobiah.

His expression as he looked at my friend was sad. "No, he can't. And I can't let him out, not yet. They've stuffed him so full of gadgets I'm not sure he's human anymore, and there's something in the middle of him I can't read at all. I think he's a walking bomb."

"But you can't read me either," I said sharply.

"With my hands I can't, but with X rays I can," he said, and laughed at my expression. "That's how I checked you for implants. Good old-fashioned X rays. Like poking your patient all over with a long needle to find out what's inside."

He was relaxed and easy again, talking to me as if I were a normal person. People usually talked to me as if I were a child, or a small animal. *Let Tobiah out,* I wanted to say. *Please let him out.* But I couldn't ask him that.

"Roder!" said Cully from the door.

The android's head snapped around as if he'd been asleep. Maybe I'd been bespeaking him after all. "What?"

"Fergus can't get us *out* of translation now."

"Coming," said the android, giving one of the dials on To-biah's tank a swift turn as he left.

The room felt smaller instead of bigger when he was gone. Left alone, I looked at Tobiah again. His pulse was still fast.

He was my only friend, if you could call him a friend. I first met Tobiah when the Sefir Zul sent me to his shop to pick up his antique bout-timer, which was being repaired. Tobiah hadn't finished fixing it, but he dug it out of a disorderly pile of other gadgets and said he'd have it ready in a couple of minutes.

I sat and waited while he worked. There was another customer in the shop, a young woman. She was lifting a clock to look at it when Tobiah said something under his breath and traced a loop in the air. The young woman stopped moving, though Tobiah was working briskly. The clocks stopped ticking. Everything stopped except Tobiah Gregg.

I didn't move. I'd learned not to draw attention to myself when things got strange. I didn't think it was a magic spell at first, because I didn't feel any pressure, but about ten minutes into the silent freeze one of his clocks ticked for the first time. It sounded like an elephant cracking its knuckles. That was when I figured Tobiah had slowed the progress of time, at least within the shop.

Slowing time was not a common skill. Like stretching space, it took the energy of a lot of magic, an accumulation of magic as big as an engine. Tobiah's familiar must be as enormous inside as my master's familiar was.

It took the customer nearly twenty minutes to finish turning the clock around to look at the price. It took Tobiah nearly an hour, an hour in which he didn't ever look at me, to finish repairing the timer. It must have been very convenient for him to be able to do that. When he was done, he made the gesture again, the customer started moving, and he presented me with the timer and a bill for the Sefir Zul. He crooked his finger, and I leaned in to listen. "Don't tell," he said without noise. I shook my head quickly, clutching the timer, and left. I hadn't moved. I hadn't breathed. I hadn't even blinked for that hour, except when he couldn't see me. How had he known? That was one of the reasons I avoided witches, because you could never tell what they would see.

I swore I wouldn't go back after that. I avoided the part of the city where Tobiah had his shop. When the square clock that hung above the main door in Zul's academy stopped working, I tried to stay out of Zul's sight, hoping he wouldn't send me, but he did. I was Zul's scholarship student, so I ran all his errands, or at least the ones that weren't important.

It wasn't as bad as I feared the second time. Tobiah smiled when I came in, looked at the clock, and said, "I can fix that while you wait. Sit here," and I sat on an old stool and watched his nimble fingers work. I passed the time by looking around for his familiar, and only when he rested his hand on it like a man caressing a pet did I realize that Tobiah's familiar was a clock, a well-worn thing of ebony, brass, and ivory. It was quiet and restful in the shop.

"Come back and visit," he said quietly as I left, so later on I did. I came and sat in his shop and watched him fix time so it ran smoothly and everything happened when it should. He never pushed on me the way other witches did. He never slowed time after that first visit. He never talked, and he never touched me, so I kept coming back, and now he was comatose in a blue tank, without his familiar. He was the only friend I'd ever had, besides my master's dog, and he didn't ever make me feel as bad as that dog did. Until now.

Now his eyes opened again, and this time it was no illusion. He was awake. "Out, out, get me out," he mouthed. *I'll get you out,* I mouthed back. *I'll get you out. I'll try.* Toby lifted his palms and pushed against the transparent cover of the tank, making his hair flow forward over his face. He made fists of the hands and pressed them on the glass so that the skin whitened in flat patches.

I ran my hands over the surface of the tank, looking for controls. There was a smooth pit the size and shape of a hand at the base, and I could fit my palm into it, but it didn't do anything that I could see. The dial Roder had turned had markings but no numbers, so I didn't know what it measured. I drew my sword and hammered the hilt on the tank, but the clear material didn't even scratch. Tobiah's face was impatient. He pressed his hands against the cover again. I put my palms up to his, and he yanked away.

He closed his eyes again, and his face went still. Though I stood with my palms on the cover for a while longer, he didn't move anymore except for the pulse.

Something soft and feathery brushed against my ankles. I looked down. The cat was there, working its front paws up and down. Its face looked less raggedy than before. I scooped it up, holding it in my arms. It purred into my face, and said, "Mine. You are mine."

"Oh." I'd thought before it was warning me off, and here it was claiming me as its own.

"Miiiine," it whispered, and butted into my chest. I stared at it in astonishment, forgetting the Sefir Zul, Rafael, and even Tobiah for a moment.

"Hey there," I said softly to it.

At the same moment I heard Fergus yell "Yes!" from the kitchen, and this time when we came out of translation, everything slid sideways and stayed on a slant, so I fell against the wall.

CHAPTER TEN

The Exchange of Parried Blows
(*Flock of Crows,* Conversation of the Blades)

The cat struggled in my arms and jumped down, crouching. It stared at me, ready to run away. A tuft of its hair floated into the air, caught in the light from the opening door.

"It's all right. I'm sorry," I said to the cat, and followed it into the kitchen. They all looked up at me. "Does this animal have a name?" I asked.

"Akamai didn't call her anything," said Electra. Her mouth was turned down. She didn't approve.

"Then I'm calling you Bear," I said to the cat, which ignored me. "Bear" after my master's dog, the one he killed.

"Whoa," said Fergus, and rolled his eyes, hastily turning his face from Roder, who ignored him. The exchange wasn't about me or the name or even about the cat herself. The name of Akamai made everyone angry every time I said it.

"You can't adopt someone else's familiar," said Cully, trying to be kind. "It's like adopting somebody's leg, or their ears. The cat will be gone in a few more days, anyway. Familiars don't survive on their own."

He was wrong. *Leave me alone, leave me alone.* "I'm not adopting her. She adopted me."

"Leave her alone, leave her alone," said Octavian in a soft singsong, his cat's eyes wide on me. Electra squeezed her mouth even more tightly.

"We know," said Cully. "We know."

Roder, who had been sitting with his face like a sad patient mask, stirred and said, "We still have a few minutes on this planet. We need to decide what to do, where to go. We can't just keep running away." They were silent. A damp breeze blew in through the window behind him. The night sky had cleared, and the stars were out.

I cautiously touched the cat's back and it—she—Bear the Younger—shoved her back against my hand in return. I never had a pet except for the dog Bear. He cared about me, he even bit my little master for me once, when little master came after me to explain something with a stiletto. He might be the master's dog, but Bear loved me. My master wasn't easy to love.

"I can't believe Enforcement has this much power," complained Electra as if she thought Roder should do something about it. Octavian began tapping his fingers.

Cully shifted, glancing at him. "Do we know they killed Julia?"

Roder shut his eyes. "Her implant went dead. I felt it."

There was a long, resentful silence. Electra glowered at the table.

Fergus blew his breath out. "You didn't promise us we'd live forever, Roder, but I thought we'd be taking Enforcement on one infraction at a time, not all of it at once. And," looking at me, "why should we believe Malka came here on her own—"

No.

"Did you find out where the Mennenkalts went?" Cully interrupted suddenly, speaking to Electra. Then he winced and shook his head.

"They were just chasing the Enforcement transport that carried out the earlier sanction, the *Hilma K. Lewis*," said Electra, startled. "I guess they're rescuing their deportees. If they followed the *Hilma K.*, they ended up off the Web. We'll worry about them later, if there is a later."

"No," said Roder, straightening up. "Fergus, try the Mennenkalt flight plan. You know how methodical and cautious they are. It won't land us inside a sun or a black hole."

They were already interrupting him.

"Ah, Roder, come on," said Cully. "Whatever might have happened to the Mennenkalts, we need to take care of our own problems right now."

And Octavian said, "If we're off the Web, how are we going to get back? Enforcement will be there before us, besides."

"Saint Jabob's salty thong!" came the voice of Fergus through the exasperated racket. "Three—four—I have a whole fleet of Enforcement ships coming in." He continued talking carefully under his breath, a Matrish litany of terms for underwear.

They were all looking at the android again, but Roder shrugged. "Where, then? Where do you want to go next? Ephrayim? Nice Sky? Vernon Two? Big Dry Pile? We either stay in the Web and let them chase us around, getting nothing done, or we leave the Web with a chance of learning something useful."

"Twelve and shock cannons," said Fergus. "Give me a destination. The drive has been fighting me like crazy. I have to start *now* if we're going to go."

Their faces were pale. They didn't want to be here, any of them. Neither did I. I wanted to be absolutely elsewhere. *Let's go,* I thought, as if it would help.

"Roder, tell us what to do," said Electra.

The android said, "Follow the Mennenkalts."

Fergus hunched over the palm jack.

Something hit the house with a loud thump.

Let's go.

Fergus closed his eyes. "The engine's doing it again," he said in a hollow voice.

Go. Get away. Get away.

Then something really hit the house. I saw a train wreck once. It was that kind of noise. Malka the Doughty in Battle stood up, flapped her hands, and squealed, *"Get away get out get out get out NOW,"* and the noise simply wasn't there anymore.

"Lords of Disorder, we're in translation," said Cully. "Fergus, I love you."

"I know you love me, but I have no idea what I did," said Fergus. "We're not even where I aimed us. We're somewhere else."

They all ignored me pointedly, and I realized I was still flapping my hands. In the silence, Roder leaned his head back and let out a long breath.

"No Mennenkalts? No Forcers?"

"Not that I can read," agreed Fergus.

Roder turned those eyes on me. For a moment, I was too

frightened to say anything. He knew what I'd done. I couldn't let anybody know what I could do. My master's orders, underlined with the gentlest touch of a razor in his small neat hand.

Roder glanced away. I breathed in.

Cully put his arms around the redheaded engineer from behind and hugged, and Fergus gave a comfortable grunt.

There was a crash outside in the hall. My ears popped, and the kitchen door thumped like a drum. Fergus said in the same moment, "We're out of translation already."

"And in vacuum, not atmosphere," said Roder. "That was the front door blowing the rest of the way out, along with all the air in the hall." He sounded as if that were nothing out of the ordinary.

Octavian got up. "Don't things explode in vacuum? What about the infirmary? What about Pegeen?"

Tobiah too, trapped awake in his tank, I suddenly remembered. Tobiah too.

Roder raised his eyebrows. "The door to the infirmary is as well sealed as this one. Pegeen's fine." I'd never been in real space before. I'd never had to be. Translation skipped that in-between stuff.

For the moment I was safe from Roder's insight. They all got to work. We were within a solar system and near a planet the engine didn't recognize, completely out of the Web. There was no organized communications traffic, Fergus said. He brought up a dark speckled screen from his console. The specks in the screen moved, and I realized he was looking outside the ship in real time at the stars. Something round swam into the middle of it, blue and white. My eyes didn't adjust right away. Then I knew what it was.

I had never seen a planet from space before, except pictures in school. The rest of them were all watching the screen too. That small thing was a whole world, suspended there in the middle of black nothing, and it made the Web seem immense, almost infinite. The Web I knew was close, border to border, a slithery pile of big balls crowded with people. This space was mostly empty and very lonely.

I felt something bump under my feet, a soundless reverberation, as if the ship had hit something. "What was that?" Electra said.

"Don't know. Automatic force field is up over the door opening and pressure's back, Electra, if you want to take a look," answered Roder.

Electra tried the door. It opened easily to her hand and she went out. "Gracious, the hall's a disaster," I heard her say and then the door shut behind her.

"Take us in closer. I want to take a look at it; it looks habitable," said Roder. "Do you know how to put a ship in orbit?"

"Orbit?" said Fergus, "Are you kidding me? Not since simulation training. Orbit. Free fall. Wow."

Cully, having taken a seat in the back of the room by himself, was talking to himself, though the others didn't stop what they were doing, nor did they seem to listen. He bowed his head, recited something in a quiet gabble, said, "Julia," clicked one of his beads, and bowed his head again. He worked through the routine again for Wladyslaw, Akamai, and some other people named LeRoy, Yannis, Cosima, Louise, Satterthwaite, Bo Dog, and Duchese Kanani Isabella. Nobody said anything to him, though Fergus bowed his head along with each name.

People did that. They mourned for the dead, like clouds regretting the loss of their rain. I would regret my own death plenty when it happened, but someone else's, no. Or maybe I would. Since earlier today—yesterday?—I hadn't been able to kill anybody. Not even Roder, who I realized was watching me again.

"That should do it," he said, shifting his eyes smoothly back to the screen. Fergus still sat staring at his tiny little screen. It was filled to the edges with blue and white now, and a black curved edge that was space. I guessed the white was clouds. I would have expected a world to be green and brown, somehow.

Roder leaned back and stretched his arms above his head. "Now, Malka," he said. "We need to talk some more."

No.

"Shouldn't we be working on a plan?" interrupted Cully.

"I am," said Roder. "I have to find out what we have to work with. I'm a Monitor. What powers do I have as a Monitor?"

Cully said, "The right to place administrative hold, the right to inspect evidence and interrogate witnesses, the right to investigate independently, the right to be informed of all Enforcement operations . . . Oh."

"That's it. Those are rights, not powers. Who grants those rights?"

Again Cully said, from some memorized text, "The government by means of the Charter." He was starting to look unsure of himself.

"No. Who tells Enforcement they have to do what I say?"

"The NeverMind."

There was a long wait while everybody got that straight in their heads. "Right. And they're ignoring the NeverMind. The only power I had depended on was the ability of the NeverMind to make Enforcement do what I wanted. Now all we have left is ourselves."

"Ourselves and Malka. Malka's a little messed up," said Cully, finished with his litany, leaning back and regarding me. All their eyes were on me again.

Stop staring at me.

With surprising suddenness they were all looking elsewhere. My head felt light.

"It's like an electric shock when she does that," said Fergus, who was back staring at his screen.

"Or a breaking wave," agreed Roder, looking down at his hands from beneath his eyelashes as if they were fascinating. "Malka, you cast spells with words so easily it's scary. You haven't known you were a speaker long, have you? You told me you weren't a witch, and you believed it."

I didn't answer. I wouldn't repeat myself.

"I bet you bespoke only when you really wanted something?" he persisted, glancing up at me. His eyes creased at the corners when he did it. "That's how most bespeakers get started."

All I ever really said to myself was *leave me alone*, and I said it now.

Roder shook his head as if to clear it. "Stop it. Please."

Cully wiped his forehead with his beads. "My mind went completely blank. What happened to Electra, anyway?"

Roder squeezed his eyes shut. "Concentrate, people."

"I'm going to see where she went," Cully said, got up, and left the room. Roder brought his hands together, leaned forward to say something more, and then Cully yelled, "Roder!" from the hall. He rose and looked out, and then went out. Cully yelled again, higher and louder. "Roder! He's trying to get into the drive chamber! Roder—"

As he stepped out, something crashed in the hall. I went to look. Roder's back was toward me. His knees were bent and his arms were in front of him. He was carefully inching forward toward someone facing him, someone who was a black shadow against the glare of planet-light through the shattered front door. Electra lay on her face in front of the drive doorway, her back slowly falling and rising. Cully was on his knees nearer to me, trying to get up.

"Malka, move please," Octavian said as he slipped past me. Slight as he was, he grabbed Cully by the shoulders, dragging him back into the kitchen.

"Malka, get him. I'll get him from this side," said a familiar, calm voice from the other end of the hall, and the silhouette moved forward. "You can do it. Run him through."

It was Tobiah. He'd gotten himself out. Or maybe I had gotten him out.

CHAPTER ELEVEN

Attack with Reprise
(*Biter's Bark,* True Action
behind False Action)

Roder didn't look behind him. He took another step forward, moving very slowly. "You know this young man, Malka?" he said.

"Yes."

Tobiah was dripping blue fluid still, and his round face looked naked. "Come on, Malka, get him for me. Kill him." Tobiah never talked to me like that before. "He works for Enforcement, Malka. He's a Forcer."

Now that wasn't right. Even after such a short time, I knew Roder wasn't exactly a Forcer. I could understand why Tobiah would think it, though.

Roder said, still moving forward, "How long have you known him, Malka?"

"You've known me for years, Malka. Who do you believe, him or me? Who do you believe? We've got to get out of here. I know how to take over the drive."

If he was Tobiah, he could make time slow down and take care of Roder himself.

"Who do you believe, Malka?" he repeated, moving closer, his eyes fixed on Roder. As he neared me he looked like a drowned man or a dead man.

He could take care of Roder himself. He could.

I heard a piece of Octavian's voice in the kitchen, hushed, and Cully's voice saying, "Electra."

"Slow time," I suggested to Tobiah. He made an annoyed face, just as he had in the tank, just as he had when I tried to warn him in his shop. He crouched and he hurled himself straight at Roder. It was all wrong.

"Now!" he yelled as he jumped.

Slow time. Slow time. Slow time.

Fergus started, "Sweet Cecil's under—" and then the voice dipped to a lazy growl and fell below hearing. The air turned to honey or hot mud or thick dust, and I had to struggle to pull it into my lungs. It felt different from the time when Tobiah did it in his shop. That felt normal, just looked and sounded funny. This felt like a very bad dream or a drowning.

Tobiah hung stopped in midair, his mouth open and his teeth showing. Both his thumbs were inches from the android's eyes, and his thin muscles stretched his naked skin like tent ropes. It was a commando's leap, coordinated and athletic, but he had already failed. Roder's hands were sweeping Tobiah's arms apart, and balanced neatly forward on one foot he was already kicking one of Tobiah's legs aside with his other foot.

Tobiah and Roder were together in their agonizing dawdle. Tobiah was moving even more slowly than the android. I had made the time drag, not Tobiah.

Something leaned against my leg. I looked down. The cat, moving normally, stared up at me with her mouth open, panting. She was in slow time with me.

When I looked up again, I could see Tobiah's eyes getting even wider, his teeth showing more. He looked like an ogre or a machine. I waded through the air to look at Roder's face. It was calm and intent. When he was this focused, he didn't look sad. Tobiah's arms were separated now, missing Roder's eyes, and the android was turning him around, using the spin he had applied with his foot.

I still had time to do something, if I wanted to. Tobiah had been something like a friend to me. Or maybe he hadn't. Slow time really didn't feel anything like what I felt in his shop. I was wheezing. The muscles that pulled the air into my lungs were hurting.

Now Tobiah had his back to Roder, and was falling to the floor. In a gradual motion like a snake going into a burrow, the android hooked his arms under the clock maker's arms and locked his hands behind his neck, and at the same time he brought his knee into the center of Tobiah's back. They were falling together now, but Tobiah was stuck in Roder's hug. His face, approaching the ground, still had the same masklike grimace. Roder had him down, safe and alive, even though Tobiah would have killed Roder without a qualm. I coughed from the effort of drawing the air in.

There was another cough at my feet, light and thin. The cat was crouching with her head down and her gums showing, trying to breathe. I kneeled down and she stared at me but didn't see me. Then she rolled to one side with her ribs pumping in and out. No. I'd never had a pet before. She couldn't die on me now. *No, no, no, faster, please, no,* I said to her.

"—pants, we're at the end of nowhere!" it sounded like Fergus said.

The time had quickened again. There was a thud and a struggle and Roder was kneeling on top of Tobiah, holding his head back and up at an uncomfortable angle. Tobiah continued to fight. His legs were kicking all over the place. "Get Octavian," said Roder to me. "I need to get your friend back in the tank. I have to keep him from hurting himself."

Even with Octavian's help it wasn't easy. They wrestled Tobiah into the infirmary and I could hear grunts and splashes. Then they came back and got Electra, not looking at me.

I understood why. But Tobiah wasn't my friend. He wasn't even a witch. I'd been fooled twice. Was there a third level to Zul's deception?

The cat bounded ahead of me into the kitchen, tail high. Fergus, oblivious, was muttering to himself and staring into his screen. Cully was leaning on the table, holding his beads to his big chest. "Is it over yet?" he asked me.

"It's over," I said. I went to the window. The imaginary wallpaper sun had started to rise, bright as the real one, and a sweet heavy smell like lilac flowed in from some flowering bushes the other side of the garden wall. The cat jumped up to the sill next to me and leaned on me, hard, her warm fur going up my nose. I snorted in annoyance and she jumped down into the garden.

"How did he get out?" Octavian said, coming in.

"I don't know," said Roder. "It wasn't broken. He got the locking mechanism to disengage somehow."

"I think I must have let him out," I said, "But I don't think he's really who I thought he was." A hand on my shoulder, hard, turning me around. Cully stopped because the tip of my blade was beneath his jaw. He lifted his chin, swallowing, but I followed his movements.

"You forgot what I said about touching me," I explained to him.

"Cully," said Roder.

Cully took a deep breath. Roder watched us and did nothing to stop me. I let the weapon drop, and noticed it was still smeared with the Forcer's blood, mostly dry now. I scratched at it with a fingernail.

"Roder, you won't believe it," said Fergus, still staring into his screen. "I was trying to get a fix on our absolute location, and I can't map us. We're so far outside the Web there aren't any standard beacons—" Still talking, he had turned excitedly to Roder and stopped. Everybody in the room excepting himself and Octavian looked as if they had just survived a tornado.

"Where did Electra get to?" he said. "What happened?"

"She's in the infirmary tank," said Roder. "The boy in the tank got loose and gave her a concussion. I had to wrestle him down. I sedated him, but I think you're right, Malka, and whoever he is, he's not a witch either. While he was conscious the instruments didn't even jiggle, until you did what you did."

Roder was rummaging in a cupboard above the refectory console. He pulled out a white cloth and tossed it at me. I caught it by reflex and realized he was giving me something to clean my sword. Bribing the bad dog, I thought to myself, but I sat down and started to use it. Tall Cully still stood there gloomily staring at Roder just out of my blade's length. He looked like his feelings hurt all over.

"Leave her alone, Cully. She told you not to touch her, didn't she? And she didn't stop me from taking the boy down when she could have. She had plenty of time. Come on, Cully, come on, I'll take care of that arm." Cully's shoulders didn't relax, but he turned slowly toward the android.

He had seen me in that long instant when I slowed the time. Roder had seen me.

"I'm sorry," I said.

He gave me such a sweet smile it made my teeth hurt.

"Stop that," I said, and his smile widened. I was going to get off this ship. He was dangerous.

"You resist my charm? Deep woman," he said, and took Cully out to the infirmary.

It wasn't hard to get the dried blood off the shiny surface of the blade. I worked in silence, as I had most of my life. Roder had asked me if I talked to myself when I really wanted something. Most of my life I didn't want things much. Mostly I wanted people to leave me alone, and Roder wasn't leaving me alone.

Of course when I was little I did want something badly. I wanted to leave my little master, wanted to run away, wanted to escape his slim-fingered clutch. That was all I really cared about. And when I wanted something badly, I did something about it. I ran away from my master and stowed away on a ship that looked like this one. I went to Caliban and found the Sefir Zul. No magic spells required. As simple as that.

Well, Caliban was not exactly simple. It had seemed simple to begin with. I did some research, and I chose Caliban on its reputation. It was as grouchy as they said, but it had the best martial arts center in the Galaxy, so that's where I went. I didn't realize that like most worlds these days, they trained only their own people. When I arrived, it took me weeks of going around to every dojo and salle I could find before I gave up. The sword-teachers were grim and silent and none of them would take on a newcomer.

So I found myself a job as an errand runner, and settled down to wait until I wasn't a newcomer anymore. I wanted to be a fighter badly, very badly indeed, but I didn't talk to myself, didn't cast any spells. I just waited. It was before I came fully awake, so waiting for weeks or months or even years wasn't a problem.

While I was waiting, the Sefir Zul found me. He was one of my regular drops. I delivered uniforms like the one I was wearing now. If he was my last job for the day, I would stay by the doorway watching his students. If anyone caught me looking, I could slip out fast. I loved the noise of the people crossing swords. I loved the movements of the fighters. Zul taught his students to dance the game, and they didn't know it.

One day, Zul caught me looking, but I couldn't slip out because he was standing in my way, towering over me. He looked down at me from under his caterpillar eyebrows and then he watched his students instead, but he still didn't move from the doorway. He stood there a long time. I could smell him all the while. When he moved into the room as if he had forgotten me, I slithered out, my heart pounding. The next three times I made my deliveries and escaped. The next time, feeling safer, I stopped to watch again, but Zul caught me again, and he forced me to stay again. He did it again and again, until one day when I stopped to watch, it was a Wednesday and a new class was starting. When Zul was handing out uniforms, he threw one to me. I stayed and learned. I felt like an alien, but things worked out—I thought. I hoped Zul didn't know what I really was. I hoped he thought I was a little witch with a hair-trigger temper, just the way Roder did.

My little master still controlled me, no matter how far away I ran. He ordered me never to let anyone know what I really was, so I never did. And I never would. He didn't really need to use pain on me to make sure of that, but he liked doing it.

The blade was clean now. I didn't really need to keep polishing it the way I was. I slid it into the scabbard with a hiss. The cloth was smeared red-brown. I folded it up into a small wad, but I didn't know where to put it so I set it neatly on the table in front of me.

I could not believe I was so naive, after all this time running and hiding. Tobiah was not my friend. I should have known. The Sefir Zul was not my hero. The Sefir Zul was an Enforcer, one who could order another Forcer to sacrifice his arm. No wonder that poor Forcer in the school had looked so frightened, reciting his nonsense about magic suppressors. No wonder Zul had chastened his student when he mocked the Forcer. And Tobiah was not a witch. And he was not my friend. Was he part of Zul's plan? Had I been sent to Tobiah so I might think him a witch, and free him when Roder captured us both? Were all the

Sefir's students Forcers too? No, that was too complicated a
web for one small grim Malka with a bad taste in her mouth.
Malka the Sleepless, Malka the Rumpled, Malka the Flapper of
Hands.

CHAPTER TWELVE

The False Parry
(*Dick Johnson*, Defending
What Is Not Attacked)

Some time later, something smelled like grilling sausages. Octavian was sitting opposite me at the table eating a thick sandwich with both hands. The others were leaning against the wall near the door, talking in muted voices. I heard Cully say, "You know, like when you're trying to pick up a mouse and it sinks its little teeth into you. It's such a shock, even if it doesn't draw any blood."

Fergus laughed up at him, but Roder said, "Not a mouse. Think of a sparrow hawk, maybe, if that makes it easier." Cully loomed over the other two like a pigeon in a group of sparrows himself, but there was no doubt who was leader there: the slim sad android leaned back against the wall and they arranged themselves on either side of him. All his people acted as if they were in love with him.

I got up and walked over to the food console. The men fell silent when I approached. As I feared, the only control was a palm jack.

"Could I have some food too?" I said to them. There was a time I didn't need food.

"Sure," said Roder. Cully, expressionless, moved forward and I moved back to give him room to work. He gripped his beads in his off hand to ward against me while he did it. Humans and their talismans, setting magic to catch magic. That was why I was in such a mess.

I took my food back to the other end of the table to eat. I was giving them space, since they didn't want to talk near me, but their conversation had ended and they all got something to eat as well. Roder stayed leaning against the wall, his worn blue shirt creasing between his folded arms.

"Octavian, you're sure the planet has no mind of its own?" he said quietly.

Octavian finished his mouthful. "It has concentrations of magic here and there mumbling to themselves, but nothing I recognize as a Cybernal. Nothing large enough or clear enough." He tore off another mouthful.

"Magic doesn't organize itself. That tells me there's human presence on the planet and they have talent."

Octavian stopped chewing. "A renegade world?"

The others looked away as if he had said something embarrassing. It was the witch's daydream, the inspiration for all kinds of stupid insurrections, the Eden where the talented could play witch without persecution. My master and his associates—not his friends, he would have no friends—had talked of it as if it were a certainty. To me, it sounded like a nightmare, a world all full of witches, all poking and prying and pushing on me.

"Possibly," said Roder. "They do exist, you know. Usually not for long if there's a trail to follow, but the Web is a bigger place than most people imagine. I don't know how the Mennenkalts got these coordinates in the first place unless they set the world up themselves. I would have sworn they never went off-planet."

"But these aren't the coordinates the Mennenkalts gave in their flight plan," said Fergus. "I thought I told you. We're somewhere else completely."

Silence.

"We're lost?" said Octavian.

Roder finally lifted his head. "Well, no wonder they weren't here when we arrived. Malka, where are we?"

"You're asking *her*—" began Fergus.

I shook my head.

A thump, a crash, and then another crash came from the hall. Octavian stood up suddenly, saying, "The drive is screaming." The android ran to the door and went out. "Malka!" he shouted.

He was standing at the broken door of the drive, covering his face with his hands and peering through the fingers. I came and stood at his shoulder. I saw what Roder couldn't see, and I said, "I didn't let him out this time."

"My fault," he said grimly. "I should have checked. He reset it for self-release when he got out. Can you see him? Is he still alive?"

"Sort of."

The room was as empty and silent as ever, except that Tobiah sat cross-legged in the center. Tobiah, or something from which Tobiah's face and body hung like an ill-fitting suit. He was obviously as blinded by the drive as Roder was, and his skin was crawling. I'd seen that happen before; the compressed magic was changing the stuff he was made of. He didn't seem to mind. His face was as still and empty as it had been when he was in the tank. "Tobiah," I said. He lifted his head and turned it this way and that, searching for the source of the noise. Then he opened his mouth wide, and shoved two fingers of one hand down his throat and leaned forward, making a coughing, strangling sound. A small sphere was the only thing that came out, a shiny cold sphere the size of a walnut. It bounced on the floor in front of him and lay still. He looked at it.

He held it between his nimble clock maker's fingers, cracked it open, and stared at what was inside.

Then his skin melted away like a pile of sand in a high wind, starting with his hands and face, peeling away and leaving behind an opalescent stick figure with Tobiah's blue eyes. The opalescent figure began to get to its feet.

A chilly breeze blew past me from the chamber. It wasn't a breeze, it was the cold I felt when I went near one of the new Enforcement ships. The stuff drifting out of the sphere was blackmatter. It killed live magic.

No, no, no. The escaping waves of magic from the terrified engine broke over me, roaring. If you wait for just the right moment, if you go loose and stay open, you can ride on top of a breaking wave. It feels like being in an earthquake or a high-speed accident, and it is as hot as an explosion.

A quiet voice came from the kitchen: Fergus, shaking. "Roder, we're losing the drive. It was screaming, and now it's fading away somehow, like water going down a drain." Around and around and around, down the drain.

"Well, then, take us down. Fergus, take us down," said Roder in a voice so calm, it felt like the end of the world, or the beginning. He disappeared through the shattered door of the infirmary; I heard shattering. Blue fluid flowed out the door on the floor, and he splashed out supporting Electra and Pegeen. Both of them were half-asleep. Pegeen's abdomen was nearly healed already, though a pink stripe went from one hipbone to the other. Fergus was already bent over his console. "Prepare to evacuate, people," Roder said, leading the way to the door.

"Evacuate?" said Cully.

"The moment we touch down. Run as fast as you can, as far as you can. Everything in the ship is held together by the drive."

The floor shook and we bounced. "We're down. Petrus!" said Fergus. I thought it was another swearword, but he ran past us to dive into his bedroom, resurfacing a moment later with an enraged-looking parrot clinging grimly to his shoulder. They crowded past me heading for the front door, Cully clutching his beads, Octavian holding his pendant, as if their familiars were all the baggage they needed.

Where was the cat? Unsteady on my feet, I went to the window. She was sitting washing herself on the garden wall. "Hey," I said. She swiveled her ears at me and kept washing.

I climbed over the sill and dropped down. The grass was high and damp, and my slippers were wet the moment I landed. The cat jumped and whirled to face me. "Bear, we have to go," I said, wading toward her, reaching my hands out. She crouched, her hindquarters up, her eyes staring. "Don't run, puss," I said, slowing down and reaching out to her.

"Malka!" Roder's voice from the window startled the cat, and she jumped down on the other side of the wall. I climbed over after her. She had her back to me and her tail twitching.

"We have to go now!" Roder said. She crouched again but didn't move. I bent my knees as I approached her, reaching out and calling her name.

"Malka, come now, please," Roder said just as softly and just as gently as I was talking to Bear.

She twitched her tail one more time, and then I had her. I was clutching her around her middle and holding her to me while she tried to climb off me with every claw. I rolled over the wall and ran to the window.

It was too high to reach, but Roder was still leaning out of it, stretching his arms down. I didn't want to let go of the cat. I held her to me with one arm and reached up until he caught my fingers. It hurt worse than when Cully had caught me. Halfway up, the whole world went boom and I could hear rocks falling off the top of the garden wall behind me. I scrambled over the sill with Roder's help into the empty kitchen. Everyone was gone. Something soft smacked me in the back of the head, a clod of dirt. Dirt and grass sprayed past us from the window.

"Come on," he said, and we ran down the hall and out the door, burst into an open plaza between tall buildings, and kept running. A hundred yards ahead, I saw the crew standing and watching us, Octavian supporting Pegeen, Electra with her arms hanging over the shoulders of Fergus and Cully. "Run! Go!" shouted Roder, flinging his hands out as if releasing birds, and the crew obeyed him. They kept going until they disappeared over the neatly paved crest of a hill. From the square openings of a big red building, people were coming and looking out.

A crack and a roar like thunder sounded behind us and echoed off the buildings. Roder slowed to a walk and turned around. The cat seized the opportunity to jump away from me and land. Her tail was lashing.

There was another crack, and more thunder, and the house shook, and another crack, and then the windows blew out. Seven crows burst cawing out with them, leaving feathers swirling behind, and rocketed toward the horizon. With a crash, the frame of the front door fell forward, and an opalescent stick figure leapt out and ran past us, blue eyes staring and mouth open, the hand that had been inside Tobiah-puppet.

Behind him a solid fountain of earth and rocks poured out of the apertures, which held for a moment and then began to crumble outward. The sides of the house were buried in dirt, rising higher and higher. Then an entire side of the house bulged out and a black clump of tree roots thrust into the air, followed

by the rest of the tree, the pine tree outside my bedroom. The
other side of the house simply tore off, and more trees fell out.
Then the roof, making a groaning sound, began to rise, wob-
bling, into the air, propelled by a crumbling mound of clay and
topsoil. The house disappeared, covered by the geyser of soil,
except for the roof, which like a hat was perched atop the growing hill. Finally, the roar began to subside, and streams of mud
bubbled from the sides of the earthen mount, joining at the base
into a clay-colored stream that spread out over the square and
rippled over the hill going away from us. Fish flopped and jumped
in the shallow stream.

"I always wondered what would happen to the scenery if the
drive went," said Roder.

CHAPTER THIRTEEN

The Engagement of Blades (*Birdy's Clasp, Suspicious Embrace*)

A clod of dirt landed a few feet away and rolled toward us, stopping a few inches away with roots sticking out of its underside.

"I guess we're marooned for the moment," said Roder calmly, prodding with his toe at it.

Some of the people coming out of the red building were arguing with one another, shaking their arms at one another so the bright sleeves trembled. Two, gaudy robes swirling, were walking toward us. The nearest of the crowd, a broad-faced bearded man swathed in magenta, shouted something at us, something that pushed against me. I wriggled my shoulders in irritation, said *I am not here*, and began to walk in the opposite direction. The cat too leapt into motion and bounded ahead of me, but then skittered off to one side and disappeared. A moment later she sauntered out again and sat down, letting me pass her by, and then cantered past again. "Malka!" I heard Roder call. I looked back. His expression was wary, he was leaning as if he wanted to walk, but he wasn't moving and the first of the colorful gentlemen was almost upon him. They were witches, then.

I watched for a moment. It wasn't my problem.

Roder isn't here either, I said anyway.

The natives came level with Roder and went past, making harsh comments, huddling around an empty spot on the pavement, and grasping at air with their hands. He backed away from the group as they began to snarl at one another.

I saw in my head the red blotch on the neck of the Sefir Zul, and Zul's face, the expression on the android's face in the corridor when I faced him with the blade he had handed back to me.

Cully's face, too. I was coming apart at the seams, sparing people, saving people like this. It was bound to happen. *Not yet, please, not yet.*

I looked around me. The street was narrow, winding, bumpy, and deserted. The houses on either side gaped empty. If you could call them houses. The street was like an amusement park, or a museum, because each one was odder and more beautiful than the next: encrusted glass mosaic next to limestone arches next to carved marble inlaid with wood, all of them different heights and widths.

I was going the opposite direction from the one Roder's crew had taken. He would follow them and I would be free from them all, and from the troublesome way they made me feel.

The air smelled of dusty resin and a tarry, dark tang I recognized after a while as wood smoke. The houses stayed absurd, but they got smaller. Then I crossed an invisible dividing line: the road straightened, and the houses became nearly identical bungalows, sane, smug, and boring. The smoky smell intensified, and then a nagging whisper of sewage. That was another odor you rarely found on Web worlds, though humans always smelled far stronger than they knew.

The cat passed me again, tail up, her soft feet pacing lightly, went diagonally across the road in front of me, and disappeared down an alley. Two houses later, she trotted out and cut across my path, looking intent. At least one companion had stayed with me.

I turned left at a fork and continued downhill, slowing to a walk. The staid villas gave way to rows of less substantial houses, some of them with peeling paint and injured dignity. There were people here, sitting on the steps, talking in groups, not staring at me because I *wasn't there*, after all. I saw no cars, and the people's palms were smooth, no sockets. It really was a world outside the Web. Enforcement wouldn't know where I was. My empty-eyed master wouldn't know where I was, then. I was safe here. I could live here.

If I was staying, I needed more people than this. I needed a busy tavern, or a roof-raising, or a party, some place where people talked and talked and I could sit and soak up the words. Farther down the hill, perhaps.

Behind me, someone made a chirping noise. I ignored it, but the cat, ahead of me, cocked her ears back and sat down in the road. As I passed her, the chirping came again. I glanced back, and saw Roder a few paces behind, scooping the cat up into his arms and scratching with one finger behind her ears.

I am not here, I insisted.

"The rest of my crew has implants. I can find them when I want them," he said vaguely to a spot just past my right shoulder, catching up and walking even with me. "They'll find me."

Malka is not a member of your crew.

He strolled along holding the cat for a few steps, then shook his head. "It's remarkable that you can do that to me. I told you I'm shielded against magic, didn't I? You bespeak me so strongly that it takes a few moments for my shield to recover. It's as strong as what that whole pack of Talents were just doing before you rescued me up the hill."

Was there nothing I could do that he wouldn't notice?

He continued, "Did you know that you have grown about two inches taller some time in the last hour?"

No. I broke into a run, startling a young woman who was just opening her front door so that she jumped back and slammed it. I ran to the next cross street and swerved left, then cut back up the hill on the next turn. I could run like this for hours if I needed to. I passed a man trudging up the hill holding the hands of two small children, and they all turned to look.

"I *am* an android, I *can* keep up with you," said Roder from next to my elbow, and I yelled and drew my sword. He backed away just enough for me to miss him every time the flailing edge cut past. His footwork was really wonderful, some part of my mind commented. Meanwhile, the calm-eyed cat watched me from his shoulder, and the man I had passed picked both children up by the midsection and escaped, the children giving high thin complaints.

"You're not going to kill me. You're not the murdering type."

"I've killed millions," I hissed, and put some shoulder into my attack.

"Lately?" He leaned back out of the way, taking another step back.

I was found out. He knew. I dropped the blade and stood with it hanging from my fist, glaring at him.

He smiled that sweet smile, a genuinely happy one. "I like you," he said. "You interest me. One of the disadvantages of a long life. After a while, you don't run into really interesting people anymore. I'd hate to pass up the opportunity to get to know you better."

I closed my eyes. When I opened them again, he was still there. He did look interested. The river-colored eyes had a distant sparkle in them, and he wasn't sad at all.

"I am not a member of your crew."

"No."

"I am not a witch."

"If you say so."

"I can't help you."

He shrugged and fell into step beside me. Somehow, we were walking down the hill again. The man and his children peered at us from behind a house. I saluted them gravely with my sword and sheathed it. Malka's Surrender, as painted by a second-rate half-blind artist for a memorial picture commissioned by a fourth-rank office of the civil government, to be hung in an unused corridor. Everything had gone from bad to worse to calamity today, but there was no point in struggling. I could escape him later.

He put the cat down and it sat and washed while we passed it, but I knew it would catch up. Now that he mentioned it, my beautiful new armor was tight on my chest and shoulders. I had always been a growing girl, but the food had been rich today.

The odor of smoke and poor drainage intensified. We turned left, then right, and then we walked into the midst of a full-blown market. Ramshackle wooden buildings spilled out their contents on jury-rigged shelving. Leaning into the street were rough-built stands and half huts bulging with shoes, fly-ridden meat on ice, toys, spices, and frying dough. People were lined up shoulder to shoulder reaching for things or working their way through the crowds, and banging one another with their string bags and baskets. The stink was rich and complex: well-aged garbage, fish, urine, resin, sweat, sawdust, the metallic tang of meat and overripe apples, and a sweet reek of caramelized sugar.

In the middle of the road, a man squatted on a loose-woven blanket next to a carved wooden model of a skeleton and a pile of water-smoothed rocks. He saw us between the people, raised one weather-beaten hand, and called something to Roder. The android shook his head and kept going through the crowd.

I couldn't see the cat anywhere, and when I looked around for her I saw the squatting man beginning to rise. I started to walk faster, snaked between a woman as wide as a milk cow and a bent man counting out coins to her, and heard someone shouting behind me. I ducked and burrowed under somebody's arm. I found myself in Roder's shadow again.

People were speaking to him and nodding to him as he passed, saying the same thing the man on the blanket had: "Bielo, Bielo, Bielo?" Roder kept shaking his head, and I watched their faces get doubtful, one by one. Another shout came from behind us. Roder led me in between two fruit stands and out into the street. The cat skittered out after us.

Roder stopped and laughed. "Thought I felt a beacon." We were facing a house with a porch, shutters, and a paneled front door. The house had started out small. The base had been built upon sideways and upward, with wood, stone, slate, and straw. A roofed walkway of weathered wood led to something in the back, probably stables from the smell. Over the door hung a heavy wooden sign painted with many coats of enamel. There was a second story and an attic, and it was all painted a crumbling white, but the original house had looked exactly like Roder's ship. A Monitor's ship.

"I have a brother here," said Roder, and entered. I could hear footsteps behind us.

Inside the tavern—it was obviously a tavern, smelling of food and sour beer—a man behind the bar looked up. Here, yes, was Roder's brother.

"Hello, Bielo," said Roder.

"Roder. I knew it was too good to last," the man, or rather the Massim-model android, answered in Standard, putting a mug down. He was not Roder. He was thicker, with a small round belly pushing the waistband of his trousers down and a dish cloth flung over his shoulder. The lines at the corners of his mouth were sharp folds, and his eyes were the eyes of a man who did business. I obviously had to adjust some of my notions about androids if two identical models could be so different. "Were you the thunder earlier?" It was his name the people had been saying outside, then, the name of another cinestar from the twenties.

Roder lifted his eyebrows. "Thunder?" People were crowding into the room after us, curious and loud. The cat had disappeared again.

"There was a big noise and half my mugs fell off the wall."

"Oh. My drive blew and the scenery turned inside out," answered Roder.

Bielo got a mug down. "You're marooned here too, then? Have a drink? And a drink for your little Forester? Where'd you get her, anyway? I thought you hunted them all down a long time ago."

Hunted them down?

Roder flicked his eyes at me. "Ask her yourself."

"Oh. My apologies, madam. I'll give you a drink, Roder, but I can't help you."

Roder leaned forward on his elbows. "Bielo, it's full-scale war now, not just government politics. Enforcement is trying to take over the Web." The room was full now, and noisy with conversation and laughter in the language I didn't know. A man was talking to my back, tinny and insistent.

Bielo raised his voice. "That may well be, but I still can't help you. I don't have a drive. This is a witch world. When I found it, nearly ninety years now, I set down right where I am now to have a look around. In less than half an hour the local Talents happened by—"

The man's voice behind me got louder. I turned in irritation. It was the skeleton man from the road, and he was asking me something about Roder, jabbing his finger at him. Three other people stood behind him, their faces eager with inquiry. I shook my head and turned back.

"—zoning violation of some kind. They sucked the drive hollow, and did it without blowing my space-fold pockets. I don't know where the scenery went. When I came back I had to pretend I was a local squatter and I put my crew to work in the kitchen until they learned the language. I've been here ever since. Actually, I'm the great-grandson, as far as the locals know."

The skeleton man was repeating himself louder, as if that would make me answer him.

"I understand," said Roder. "Can you at least house us for a day or so?"

"I'm a businessman. I need my rooms. I'm always right on the edge as it is."

The native poked me in the ribs from behind, and I jumped off the stool to face him. He flinched back, and then laughed down at me, showing a mouthful of stained but healthy teeth.

"Malka, don't," said Roder quietly. "Bielo, she's very cranky when she's pushed. I need to get her out of this crowd. And you're still government."

"The government's awful small and awful far away; I bet Enforcement's taking care of everything just fine. And if you're stuck here like me, money's tight. I'd give you and your lady friend a room, but I'd have to ask you to help me out."

The skeleton man stepped forward and poked his finger down at me again, saying something different now. I put my hand to my hilt.

"Malka, don't, please. Bielo, I'm not staying long if I can fix this, but I promise I'll help if I'm stuck here. I invoke your contract."

The skeleton man poked me in the middle of the chest, squatting to do it, and laughed. Then he looked down in amazement at my blade, which was touching the hollow of his scrawny throat. The room was silent.

Bielo moved slowly, hands up. "I'll see what I can do. Make her drop that, all right? The man's harmless, and a good chiropractor to boot."

"And I need the language if you can give it to me. Not her. Implants don't work on her. Malka?"

"He was poking me," I explained. Roder sat there with his

arm on the bar, looking at me with the tea-colored eyes as if we were old friends and he'd heard it before. The other Massim, with his hands half extended, was a stranger whose eyes were flat and anxious. Roder cocked his head, I put my blade back, and the skeleton man bared his brown teeth at me in a nervous grin. I bobbed politely at him, and he bobbed back at me.

The room Bielo gave us was tiny, with a stained bed in a rope-hung frame that took up half the floor. It was obvious why Bielo begrudged us the space from the noises either side of us: loud conversations, splashing water, rhythmic thumps, and occasional moans. Bielo wasn't exactly running a hotel. He got his money's worth out of those rooms, and we were taking an entire room's income for the rest of the day. I felt the bed with my hand, looked at it dubiously, and sat on the floor instead with my back to the wall.

Roder laughed and slid down to sit against the door himself, stretching his legs out so his feet nearly touched mine. They weren't actually touching, though. The man knew exactly what I could stand. It took him only a few hours to know me when no one had ever known me before. I closed my eyes to stop the feeling that the room was moving . . . Bielo said Roder had hunted all the Foresters down?

I opened my eyes again. Roder was watching me. We stared at each other in the dark room for a long time until I closed my eyes and closed the contact. *I am very very boring,* I said, but didn't open my eyes again to see if it worked. I didn't want to know.

CHAPTER FOURTEEN

Pretense of Trust (*Gorm,*
The Feint of Innocence)

I woke with a start when someone knocked on the door, and found myself halfway to my feet with my hand reaching for my sword, and Roder's hand clamped around my forearm to stop me. There was a brief scuffle, which I realized I would have lost if I'd kept going. I rubbed my arm. He didn't apologize.

"I did a copy of my language center," said Bielo, when Roder let him in. The landlord's hair was even more rumpled. "I don't know how good it is. The equipment's pretty old. I won't apologize for the vocabulary. You're getting ninety years' worth of slang and curses."

Roder turned the small thing over, then lifted the hair behind his ear. There were three sockets just like the one in my hand, in a row. He plugged the implant in. He closed his eyes.

Bielo, ignoring his inattention, complained, "My customers are not pleased, Roder. This is the second time this week a woman has caused trouble in the bar, and that doesn't go over well. There's rules for women and men here, and she's breaking them just by going around looking like that, let alone hauling out her pigsticker and poking poor old Duber with it."

Roder opened his eyes again. "I think it's working, Bielo. Thank you. Yaschutt zhay, Bielo." It was a harsh language. I'd thought it was the people, but even Roder sounded ill-tempered when he wrapped his throat around the sounds.

"Not bad, not bad. You don't have to sleep on the floor. I'm spelled against vermin," he said, letting himself out.

Bielo's footsteps faded away. Roder sat down on the bed with his eyes half-open, staring at the opposite wall. "Lie down," he said. "Go back to sleep. Oh, you can have the bed if you want. It will take me a little while to absorb this."

I shook my head and leaned back against the wall. Something scrabbled in the window above my head, and the cat crawled in through the fist-sized opening between the sash and the sill. She was carrying something small and furry, which she took underneath the bed. I saw her eyes reflecting the light and listened to her crunch. "Good," she said finally, coming out to wash. She was sitting so close to me that every time she bobbed her head her whiskers brushed me. I ran my forefinger along her back. "Mine," she said. "You are mine."

"My name is Malka."

"Maallkkaa," she enunciated carefully. "I am Bear."

"Yes."

"Good," she said again. She settled with a thump against me and put her nose under her tail. I knew the android was contemplating me but I didn't look. Your opponent should never know where you are looking; you should watch nothing and everything.

He said, "I've never seen that happen. Familiars and talismans are always keyed to their makers. You keep surprising me."

I shrugged.

"You're unusual in a lot of ways. How did you come to leave Forest?" he said. "It wasn't the kind of world people left."

I considered the question, turned it around and looked underneath it, found another question hiding behind it. "You hunted Foresters down. Bielo said."

"Ah. Yes, I did, or I tried to."

I watched the cat breathe.

"I was looking for someone," he said. "Not you."

If I looked up, the clear eyes would be watching me.

"Enforcement was very upset with Forest," he said. "I came in because they were threatening to do a Class Two wipe. Some Forest witches had built themselves an unsanctioned Cybernal—it was more than just a computer, it was an engine of enormous size. The thing was incredible, powerful enough to move a world, small enough to fit in a hand, a pocket NeverMind. They were going to turn the planet into a ship, move the whole world, take it out of the Web, make it a renegade world."

Yes, they were. I had been around for that. It wasn't something I had been looking forward to.

"Something really frightened Enforcement. They started the wipe right after I arrived. Some of their own people were still on the surface when it happened. ERC barely let me lift off even though I was already in my ship." He shrugged. "They stayed frightened. I think one of them got away, the one who had the idea in the first place. Something keeps happening on different planets, an unexplained drain, just like the one that alerted us in the first place. I've been looking for him, and so has ERC, ever since," he said. "I even thought you might be him when I first saw you, but you're not." He closed his eyes and leaned back.

No, I wasn't him. I was mostly myself these days.

It was getting dark outside. The air drifting in the window smelled of charcoal, bread, cooking meat, and vinegar. The ugly language came in, with people laughing and shouting in it.

Why did I leave Forest? My master and I caught a ride in the engine of a small houseboat just like Roder's. Maybe it *was* Roder's, if he was there when they started the wipe. My master found out the wipe was coming. We ran away from home, from sandalwood, woven baskets, my master's dog, veronicas and sweet bean soup, because Enforcement was going to wipe my world. My master tied Bear up and muzzled him and made one neat thrust under the foreleg into the heart while he looked into the dog's eyes. "Not as interesting as I'd hoped, after all our years together," he said to the dying dog, wiped his knife on Bear's fur, and left him staring on the floor.

"Beautiful place, Forest," Roder said, and I jumped.

He continued with eyes shut, talking softly. "Those deep fragrant woods. With the russet trunks, and that apple-colored fog in the middle distance. And the moss, and ferns, and those round planked houses your people built in the branches. I could lie on my face down on the ground and stare into the moss, and it was just like looking down through the tops of the trees, I could see into a miniature forest with all those tiny green branches, and insects marching through the stems like bearer-beasts going through the woods. And that wind, that rushing wind bending the treetops, with that heavenly smell drifting down in the eddies. The whole world was forest, trees marching down to the edges of the beaches, trees rolling up the mountains with only the peaks showing, trees on every bump of an island, fat leafless trees covering the desert, thin short evergreens all across the tundra up to the edge of the ice caps. All those small dark people with the shy eyes." He fell silent again, with his eyes still closed.

How very odd, and what a pretty story. Why was he lying to me? I hadn't thought about my home much until today, when Roder gave me the food. I hadn't really been awake until a couple of years ago, and when I was on Forest I was too little to take much in. I tried to think about it now, but all I could remember was the same litany of pictures. My master's hands, holding a bowl of sweet bean soup and eating it, watching me hungry and tied to a chair. The dog Bear, limping. The fragrant bedstead, and my feet on the cool tile floor in some room somewhere. The Forest Cybernal. The breaking wave. The growing darkness outside wasn't as dark as the inside of my head.

Roder rubbed his temples. He lay down full length on the bed, kicking off the soft shoes he wore, and turned his face to the wall, resting his head on his arm. He was a long dark wave against the white wall, breathing steadily.

The breaking wave. My oldest memory was the breaking wave. I always thought it was a memory of my birth. I was in the water, and the wave was rising before me, approaching me. The top of it, above my head, whispered foam into the wind. The long green slope below it, veined with white, crawled up and up, curving until the whole wave sucked in its breath and became a long rolling tube, a green glass cave all around me with the sky barely visible through the roof of seawater. I was in the moment before the crash for what seemed like forever, and then all those tons of water fell into me all at once, and I swallowed them all. My master's long-fingered hands grabbed me and lifted me up while I coughed and screamed in fury, and he held me above the surface, my legs dangling. "Perfect," he said, and squeezed me so hard I thought my heart would burst. I remembered his small blue eyes watching me cough and gasp.

At least I remembered that much, though it had parts I must have filled in since then. When he held me up, for instance, I was bone dry and we were inside a big hollow room full of magic just like the Forest Cybernal, not outside at the seashore.

I got up and took my armor off in the dusk, folded it neatly, and used it for a pillow on the floor, though I laid the sword down beside me and held on to its hilt. I'd slept on plenty of floors over the years.

I slept on a floor on the first night on the first world my master and I came to after Forest. I slipped from the ship when it landed, and let my master out from the place I had concealed him, and together we slipped through the terminal and into a part of the town where there were abandoned buildings. The floor had splinters. My little master, his lips pursed, slept on a ruined couch, and I slept on the splintered floor. In the morning, he sent me out to get some food for us, but before he did, he took me by the ears and spoke to me.

"There are people out there who will hurt you worse than I ever can, Malka," he said, holding the ears tightly so I couldn't look away. "Don't trust anyone. Just get something to eat, that's all. Don't talk to anyone, they'll just hurt you. Stay away from anybody who can hurt you. Hear me?" and he lifted me by my ears and gave me a little shake. Then he gave me a bigger shake, watching me. He sighed. "You could be interesting. Pity. I need you." I remembered how torn he was when he realized Forest was going to be wiped, how much he wanted to stay and watch in spite of the danger. It would have been fascinating, he kept repeating in his dry voice as we escaped. I remembered his dog, its muzzle tied, eyes open. There were other creatures that died in our house from time to time, eyes always open.

I nodded solemnly once he put me down. I had to do everything he told me, of course, but he hadn't told me to come back this time, and he *had* told me to stay away from anyone who could hurt me, so I would take him at his word and stay away from *him*. I was awake enough for that. My ears still burning, I went back to the terminal, stole a little food, and stowed away in the engine of the next ship leaving.

I stayed away from everyone who could hurt me, stayed in the shadows, slipped from world to world invisible and asleep. After a while I realized my little master was still hunting me across the Web, always a few steps behind. I'd stayed out of his sharp grasp, until I decided to turn and fight, until I went to Caliban, until I met the Sefir Zul. It had seemed like such a good idea.

The Sefir Zul, stepping and turning, caressing me with his blows, admiring himself in the mirror and parrying my cuts. Stepping and turning, striking and blocking, dancing around and around, I swirled to the bottom and slid down the wave back into sleep—

The door burst open. Again I was standing blinking with my sword out, but Roder was in front of me. The light in the room was the color of old wood. It was dusk, and Bielo was talking urgently in a low voice.

"You didn't tell me the mages had already seen you. Two of them are downstairs asking me about my brother. Do you have the language yet? I need you to calm them down; they're mostly harmless, but they can be impossible if they think there's real danger."

"Yes. I'll go be your brother from out of town. Don't worry." Bielo ran down the stairs after Roder, who had brushed past him and was walking down the creaking stairs, smoothing his hair with both hands. I padded after them in my bare feet. It was only when I had gotten all the way downstairs that I realized I had left my sword behind. What was I thinking?

In the otherwise empty bar, Roder blinked sleepily at a gaudy pair of dandies. One of them, with ginger hair and muttonchop whiskers, was costumed in slashed pantaloons in acid green and mint. His stockings, tunic, and tubular necklace followed the color scheme with unmerciful faithfulness. The other, more muted, was a sour-looking scholar in deep crimson from his long gown to his gaiters. He likewise had a neat hoop—crimson, of course—circling his neck, and it was he who was addressing Roder in the brusque local language, made even more brusque by his manner. The other one glanced at me standing *not here* in the doorway and dismissed me without a thought.

Roder, his shoulders stooped forward and his hair standing on end, answered him in the same tongue. His voice sounded like Bielo's, but with a whine in the back of it. He was pretending to be a local. The crimson scholar answered him sharply.

Roder continued to explain. Then the green-clad man said something and made a sharp gesture that *pushed*, and they both turned to leave. Roder's shoulders sagged and he shuffled after them, still playing the part. Bielo said something tentatively, and the green one answered with one word. The door swung shut behind them. Just like that I had what I wanted, an escape from Roder. Back into the shadows for Malka, safe again from people who could hurt her. I waited to feel good about it.

CHAPTER FIFTEEN

Displacing Target
(*Canard*, Duck-Squat)

Bielo's hand fell on my shoulder while I was waiting, and I wriggled away from it. "Stay, girl," he muttered under his breath. "He can take care of himself." I didn't know what he was talking about. I wasn't going to chase after Roder, no I wasn't. No. The innkeeper went to the door and peered into the dusk, his arms folded. He turned around and looked at me. "What am I going to do with you in the meantime? What's your Talent, girl?"

I shrugged. "Don't have one."

"You're not a witch? Don't tell me—Roder wouldn't—well, the boy must have some juice in him after all."

No, no. The image of Roder embracing me flitted through my head, incongruous and startling. I had never been anyone's bed-partner. I would have scalded anyone alive if anyone had ever noticed me long enough to try. *No.*

"Well—" Bielo stood staring at me even more doubtfully, then wriggled his shoulders as if shaking something off. A head peered around the doorjamb and inquired something in a husky voice. He snapped back at it, and it withdrew.

"Not a witch. Well, you're pretty enough, but I don't have enough customers who like that sort of thing—don't look so offended, girl, I'm trying to figure out how I can help you until Roder gets himself out."

Not now. Not ever.

His face smoothed out. "It can wait," he said vaguely. He was as well protected as Roder. Another head popped into the doorway, this one belonging to a stout gentleman with curly gray hair and broken veins in his cheeks, and this time Bielo let him come in, walking back behind the bar to take his request.

Yes, Roder would be all right. And it wasn't my job to worry about it. Here I was, where I wanted to go in the first place, a place where people talked, and I would take care of my business. I scuttled sideways along the wall and ducked under a counter on the side of the room, sitting cross-legged on the sticky floor. In my black shirt and skins I wouldn't stand out in the shadow. If I was going to survive here for more than a day or two, I needed to listen to people talking for a while.

Every time I landed on a new world, I got away from the terminal as quickly as possible and found a place where people got together to talk. Then I sat down and listened in the background until I knew the language. Every world had its own way of talking. Even if they spoke something they called good Standard, the natives of a place had their own speech, their slang, their cadences and singsongs, especially these days since people had stopped roving from planet to planet. When I arrived, it was always gabble to me, but by the time I'd been in a place for a while, I could untangle the tune and sing their song well enough for my one-word style. I'd always had the ability. My master had given it to me, so I could find my way and feed wherever I was.

I wasn't going to learn good diction from the people pouring into Bielo's inn tonight, that was for sure. The harsh language sounded even harsher in their crowing voices. It was a dissonant score played on pots and pans with rocks. It had a tune, though, as all ways of speaking did. The tune got louder and louder as the evening progressed, and it was a tired and worried tune.

The turnover was considerable. No one stayed long, though I noticed that some of them returned. The gentleman with the broken veins, for instance, left and came back several times, each time coming back in to confide something to Bielo. Most of the others followed a pattern of arriving in the door, asking something of the group at large, and moving to join the first person who answered. The talk was general, someone on one side of the room answering a question from the other side, with someone in the middle interrupting to disagree with the answer, but no one took offense. They all loved Bielo, too, just as Roder's crew loved Roder. Their faces lighted up when he spoke to them, and they gathered around him as if he were a warm fire.

As the evening wore on, Bielo's several female employees went upstairs with clients less and less often, and stayed to lean in on the conversation themselves, their damp-looking tendrils of hair swinging from their earnest foreheads and their beaded bracelets clinking. Somewhere in the first hour, Bielo stopped giving them quelling looks and hand motions and surrendered to his lack of income for the evening. Somewhere in the second hour, the cat picked its way through the room, crouching here and there to bolt down scraps from the floor, and then sat under the counter with me. Somewhere in the third hour, I began to understand a few of the words.

Around midnight, something shifted in my head.

Broken-vein was back again, explaining something to a cadaverous man with a long jaw and large hands. Long-jaw agreed with him, but judging from the expressions a number of others didn't and were tired of hearing him say it.

"—I say is, there's things mages are better at, and things the rest of us are better at, and that's just the way it is, no use arguing with it," he concluded.

Long-jaw nodded. "You got it. That's it exactly. The mages, even if there aren't as many as there used to be, they've been running things this long, they should keep running things, no offense, Bielo. But you see what I'm saying, the mages have the experience."

"No," said Broken-vein, who had bought another beer every time he'd entered the tavern. "I'm not saying experience, you understand. I'm saying nature. The mage is meant to be a ruler. It's the mage who is naturally, naturally—"

"Naturally better at buggering other mages," said a swarthy man whose apron was stained with something like chicken blood, and everybody laughed. "If we're talking nature, now, you have to admit I'm right," he said with no glimmer of humor or apology, though Broken-vein was glaring at him.

"Well, it don't have to be a bad thing, they keep it among themselves, is all. Besides, we haven't gone wrong depending on them before. Look at all the things they've done for the city, they've—"

"I'm tired of looking at what they've done *to* the city, it's falling apart—"

"And I'm tired of saying you've reached your limit once again, Seth," interjected Bielo amiably.

Seth—Broken-vein—glared at him, but the swarthy man pointed out, "You did start talking about the natural order of things," and he looked crestfallen.

"So I did, so I did. Won't do any good to say I'm sorry?"

"Won't have that kind of conversation in my tavern. People start talking about the natural order, my crockery always ends up broken," said Bielo, with a glimmer of Roder's expression, and Seth looked mournfully at the inch or so left in his mug.

"Well, isn't it the rest of us who've really been running things all along? The mages haven't done anything but argue and fight duels for the last hundred years," said the deep-voiced woman, returning to the argument, and three or four voices rose at once to argue with her.

"Running things? Who says anyone in particular is running things anymore?"

"Na, na, you've got to accept that there's laws, and there's the mages making the laws—"

"If you're talking about official, the kings are the ones that run things—"

"But who advises the kings? Their mages!"

"—Their queens!" triumphantly chimed in the deep-voiced woman, and everybody laughed.

"But then what do we need mages for, anyway?" she continued.

"We don't need them," said the swarthy man. "They just happen to exist, and we have to put up with them, that's all." The laughter stopped and there was an uncertain pause.

Bielo, as he did every half an hour or so, remembered my existence, and glanced vaguely toward the counter that sheltered me, but it was much easier to distract him than it was to distract Roder. If Roder reminded me of the man with all the dogs on a leash, Bielo was lead dog of a loose pack, sniffing and running a few steps ahead of the rest, sniffing and running. A strong dog, a wise dog, but a dog nonetheless. He wasn't interested in what Enforcement was doing to the Web, just in the small doings of the local world that affected the operation of his inn.

Those doings, from the conversation, were small indeed. Though it was a planet run by witches, the witches were getting fewer and fewer, and none of them bothered themselves with the obvious uses of magic such as long-distance travel or communication.

The chatter seemed to go round and round, the complaints and assertions of people who had never had to decide anything important in their lives, people who believed the world should and could go on as it always had.

The argument about mages did one more slow lap and then slid off into a sustained complaint about an importer of foodstuffs whom everybody knew and disliked. Everybody had a different explanation for the man's nastiness even though they all agreed he was spiteful and petty, and they bickered about that for a while. Then they compared kings, and then they complained about mages again, and then they talked about a woman who had torn up the inn a few days before, apparently using magic. I acquired a basic working vocabulary and several interesting dirty words, and all of it ran around the inside of my head, squeaking and gibbering.

I would go mad from boredom if I had to stay on this world.

I had to figure out a way to get off, even if it meant going back to the Web, even if it meant my master could sniff me out again.

Suddenly I looked up, realizing the inside of my head was the only thing making any noise. The room was silent and half-empty, and the patrons who were left had mostly lapsed into morose reflection. It had never been festive, exactly. Bielo's patrons came to ease their needs rather than to entertain themselves. The ones who were left seemed to have no place else to go, and were merely delaying the inevitable rather than enjoying themselves. The same held for me, for that matter.

I slipped through the sour-smelling room and went up the back stairs.

"Girl," said a quiet voice from the bottom of the steps.

I turned.

"He will be fine," said Bielo.

I shrugged my shoulders and went into the room.

The armor didn't fit me as well as it had. Roder was right, I had grown again. The leather was tight between my shoulder blades and gripped my upper arms, the trousers barely fit over my thighs, and the overlap between the jacket and pants was much less. I struggled into it anyway, picked up my sword, and went to the window instead of the door. Bielo had seemed worried I would leave, as if it were any of his business, and I didn't want him to stop me.

I raised the sash as slowly and carefully as I could, hearing the rumbling vibrations and sure Bielo could hear them downstairs through the walls. Indeed, I heard a thud from downstairs, but it was only people coming out the front door and turning into the dark lane below us, some of Bielo's patrons leaving, still not talking. I waited a few minutes by the window but heard nothing more from downstairs.

I slid facefirst out the window and onto the low roof, squatted down, and swung myself down into the road, landing in a crouch with nothing more than a crunch of gravel to advertise my arrival. I sat down in the dirt to pull my boots on. I couldn't see any light through the cracks in Bielo's shutters.

The front door to the tavern opened only a few feet away, and a dark figure came out, turning to close and fasten the door. The figure passed close to me going toward the hill, head down in the unlit street. I didn't dare finish pulling up my second boot.

A few steps past me, the figure turned back and took a breath. "Well, all right, so maybe he won't be all right," said Bielo. "But that doesn't mean you would be of any help. You don't speak the language. You wouldn't know where to go or what to do. Go back up to bed."

The cat landed softly in the dirt behind me, and I finished pulling my boot up. "It is of no interest to me," I said. Unfortunately, I said it in my new language.

CHAPTER SIXTEEN

The Double Touch (*Suicide's Victory*, Wound for Wound)

"In that case," said Bielo with an unreadable expression in the darkness, "you are welcome to join me," and he turned and headed up the hill.

I watched him go until he was only a dark gray blur in the blackness, then surrendered. I got to my feet and followed after, silently.

The windows of the buildings on either side of us flickered dimly, if they showed any light at all. There were no streetlights. The buildings were black shadows against a black sky, and Bielo was barely visible a few feet in front of me. A backward world, indeed, though above us the stars shone stark and bright without the outside lighting. Now that I thought of it, I supposed the houses we passed had all been built by hand, with hammers and chisels and saws and sweat.

A pale light flickered up at the next corner, bobbing up and down.

Bielo shoved me in between two houses and fell down on top of me, wrapping his arms around me. "Hush, hush, hush," he whispered. "Pretend we're lovers. There's a curfew this far up the hill."

I struggled, but he was muscular despite his round hard stomach. He was warm, too. He muttered something to himself while I tried to get my hand to the hilt of my sword, but he wasn't breathing hard or straining to hold me down.

The pale light grew brighter, bobbing faster, then filled the space we were in with a milky glow.

"What's going on here?" In the light of the glowing sphere he held in his hand, the man nearly glowed in the dark himself.

113

He was dressed in a jacket and kilt of pumpkin yellow and flame red in a diamond pattern.

Bielo answered guilelessly, scrambling to his feet and clutching his hands to his chest, "Sorry, sir, sorry, sir mage, my girl and I were just—"

I kicked his shin.

"There's a curfew, boy. Close your trousers and get inside," said the mage.

"Sorry, sir mage." It sounded incongruous in Bielo's weary voice.

The light bobbed away, but the mage called back, "Tell your flirtigiggs to wear a skirt, you won't have to go outdoors to get at her sit-upon."

"Sir," said Bielo. The light, moving the shadows up and down, faded. "Thought better of him," he muttered.

Don't touch me again, I thought, a little breathless.

"Sorry," he said, as if I had spoken aloud. "Had to be done."

He set off, walking more briskly now, and somehow I was walking beside him instead of skulking behind. We were climbing upward, toward the high horizon, which was growing brighter.

"You really resisted me," he said finally.

I didn't say anything.

"Humans don't generally resist the Massim model. We're too charming."

No comment.

"I'm not hurt. Just puzzled."

I didn't answer again.

"Huh. You don't find me in the least bit attractive? Don't happen to want to smile at me and spend time with me and trust me with your life?"

I sighed.

"Then what are you doing following Roder around?"

"He's following *me.*"

"Oh. That explains why you were going to go try to rescue him?"

Shut up.

He was a black figure in the black night, his breathing steady, watching me. The Monitor Massims were a custom model, then. I supposed you had to deal with the problem of crewing the ships with wild witches somehow. The witches gave up their freedom for love. Or maybe just strong affection. That would explain the pet-dog effect they had around him.

"You actually like the stiff-necked puritan for himself, don't you?" Bielo finally said.

I guessed I did. *Shut up,* I repeated.

He turned and walked away, and I followed.

We turned a corner into a fairyland, the amusement park I'd passed through earlier that day, but now even more astonishing. Everything was glowing in faint pastels. Every ornamental cornice, every porch roof, every piece of icing glowed in lavender, rose, and lime, and the odd-shaped windows shimmered lemon yellow. He glanced back at me. "They're mostly empty, don't worry." A muddy swath of water rippled down one side of the street, the only thing marring the picture.

We walked back into the square where we had landed earlier that day, and I realized the origin of the water flowing in the road, because a boggy spring still bubbled from the side of the earthen hummock our ship had made.

There were four buildings embracing the square. We passed the first, a pile that looked as if it had been assembled by a color-blind committee. A comfortable, elegant white mansion on the right side shone with a peaceful white light. Opposite it a black tower had only a few windows near its summit, from which cold blue rays thrust forth into the night, but otherwise it was only visible as a looming shadow across the dark sky. Beyond the two of them, a red building's windows glowed deep yellow and there were shadows of people moving about behind them. My steps slowed. Bielo glanced back at me.

"He's probably in the red building. That's where they have their court and their police, such as it is," he told me in a voice barely above the level of a thought.

"What are you going to do?"

He rubbed the top of his head. "What I have to do. It's in my nature, the contract he invoked. I have to aid him if he asks for my help, no matter what I said. Stay here." He trudged toward the front door, his shoulders down, looking less and less like Roder with every step. Roder wouldn't drag his feet on his way to an unwelcome task. He'd lift his head up and look around him with interest, accepting the job with fascination, pleased not to be bored for a change.

Bielo walked up to the front door and in, and it closed behind him. Stepping carefully and quietly, I walked across the square to the dark red building myself. There were no shadows walking across the yellow windows now. It was silent. I stood on my tiptoes to peer in a window. There didn't seem to be anybody inside, though the light illuminated every corner of the room. I dropped down again, looked down at my feet in the darkness, looked around me. No one on the broad front steps. I fit my toes in the grooves between the stones of the wall and, clutching the sill with my fingertips, pulled myself up again. I wriggled through the window. The light dimmed slightly. I slithered to the floor with a scraping noise and crouched, trying not to breathe loudly.

The light stayed dim but nobody called out, no doors opened, there were no footsteps. It was a meeting room with stepped rows of wood benches facing the center and windows in the outer wall. There was a door that led into another meeting room, this one much larger, a wide hall full of stone benches with a raised podium at one end. It was empty too, but it felt stuffy and I was uneasy, as if a large hand was pressing down on me. It smelled of smoke and the aging funk of people. The benches were littered with bits of clothing, books, and food.

There was a thump in the room I had just left, and I crouched next to the nearest bench. "Malka?" said a breathy voice. I stood up again.

Perhaps pets were not an unmixed blessing.

I worked my way between a row of benches. There were doors all along the walls, most opening into tiny meeting rooms, each one smelling of humans. The yellow light seemed to come from everywhere and nowhere, and every time I opened a door the room darkened slightly within.

A door in the corner, bigger than the rest, led into another small meeting hall. When I opened it and walked in, more stuffy pressure flowed over me from within. This room was like an amphitheater, with a balcony circling above and ranks of stalls below descending to a small round stage. In the center of the stage, on a tall stool, sat Roder, his hands folded in his lap. His eyes flickered at me and flickered away.

"Not such a good idea," he said vaguely to the air above him, and I heard a click. I turned back and saw that the door had closed behind me.

CHAPTER SEVENTEEN

Redoublement (*Scolding Sharon, Renewal of Failed Attack*)

"What isn't such a good idea?" said an elderly voice from above.

"That question. You keep asking it, but I can't answer it. 'What mage made you?' is like asking 'When did you stop beating your wife?' "

"Mages aren't permitted to marry," said another voice, dry and light. It sounded as if they were sitting in the balcony directly above me. The stairs to the balcony were on the opposite side of the room next to another door, and they probably couldn't get there in time to catch me. I took another step back.

"That was probably his point," said the harsh elderly voice. "And I have not stopped beating my apprentice. You say no mage made you. Yet you are demonstrably a made thing, an automaton. Who then made you?"

I reached for the door handle and tried to turn it. It didn't move. I looked at Roder and found his face pinched with worry. He kept talking. "A company grew me. On another world."

"Are you uncomfortable answering that question?" inquired the old man.

"It is not the answer or the question which makes me uncomfortable," answered Roder awkwardly.

"He's resisting the truth spell, Master Prosper," said the young man.

The older mage, Prosper, said slowly, "What disturbs you?"

Something scratched on the outside of the door and made an inquiring meow. I rattled the door handle.

"What was that?" said the youth. I heard footsteps above me.

"My friend disturbs me," said Roder sadly, not moving his hands from his lap.

Feet appeared on the stairs, a slim, athletic body clad in soft rose, with a speckled rose neckring, and a young man's round face peering my way. "If that is your friend, she disturbs me also," said the face. "There's a grim little wench down here, master." He pulled at his neat little mustache and stepped down farther.

I pulled my sword out slowly and waded through the pressure of the room toward him. Roder rolled his eyes and then shut them.

"Wench?" said the older voice.

"Not a local girl, I think, unless the town maidens have taken to wearing entire cows and waving knives about," said the young man, jumping the last few steps and coming forward. He ran up the aisle between the rows of seats, watching me confidently and rubbing his hands together. I extended my arm and aimed the point at his viscera, advancing more slowly. He threw his hands at me as if spraying me with water. It made me itchy so I straightened my arm slightly. He stopped a fraction of an inch before he impaled himself, with a startled expression, and tried to sweep the blade aside with his arm. With a squeeze of my fingers, I pinked the arm neatly on the way past and returned the tip to his midsection.

"Yefim?" said the voice.

Yefim didn't say anything. He smiled tightly, his chest rising and falling. He revolved his hands on his wrists, said, *"Avert,"* and stepped forward confidently.

His thin little spell didn't even give me a hiccup. I was holding the blade out in the Jesup Line, something I learned and forgot early in my training. The Jesup is limited in sword-fighting, mostly used to break your opponent's rush so that you can take over the attack. Most sane people don't choose to stab themselves. The line is weak otherwise, because of the rigidity of the arm. It's too easy for your opponent to beat your blade aside. This was the first time I'd seen someone run himself onto the Jesup, and at walking speed too.

He stopped again when it had gone in a quarter inch, tried to take a breath, and realized that the rising of his chest would widen the slit.

"Yefim!" said the voice.

He opened his mouth to answer, and realized that speaking would do the same thing. His lips curved into an apprehensive smile.

Footsteps above. "Rot you for a clot of frog's eggs, Yefim! Answer me."

Yefim shuddered and stepped back smoothly, a stain darkening his rose tabard, but I pressed him, my arm still extended, and he moved back, step by step back down the aisle toward Roder.

The rose boy came to a stop at the edge of the small stage, looking as if he'd abruptly backed into a wall. With his chin shoved into his neck, he raised his hands and said, "No, please, lovely lady, I can go no farther."

"What are—" The man coming down the stairs in a sweep of silver robes had a curly mass of gray locks, heavy-lidded eyes, and a sharp-angled parrot nose. While I was looking up at him, Yefim inhaled sharply, slid sideways away from my point, scraped it across his chest, and leaped into the first row of seats, stepping over the backs to climb several ranks up. "How did you get this far?" said the old man to me.

"She walked," said Roder, his eyes still closed. "That's what she does. She walks into trouble."

With my eyes on both of them, I backed toward Roder.

"What are you doing?" inquired the old mage, cocking his head with baffled interest.

"Can you move?" I said to Roder.

"I'm tied up," he answered, wiggling his fingers as if it should be obvious to me.

"With what?" He didn't answer me. I lifted his right hand off his lap. It went up just fine. He watched it as if it belonged to someone else.

"Ah," said the old mage, sitting down on the stairs. "Armed and shielded from magic. Lovely. Are you someone's fetch? Whose?" He revolved one wrinkled hand in an irrelevant gesture that made my elbows itch, and Roder squinted in pain.

Yes, I was someone's fetch, but he wouldn't be acquainted with my master. I lifted Roder's other hand. They both stayed in the air.

"No, hm. Did you arrive with that exploding house, then?" Another gesture, this one requiring both hands. Roder averted his head from me. His shoulders tensed.

I put down my sword, grabbed both of Roder's hands, braced my foot on the lower rung of the stool, and pulled. Nothing.

"Are you a daemon? A conjuration? A clockwork monster like your friend?" The old man raised both hands into the air so that the sleeves of his robe slipped down to his elbows. Roder cried out, tipped forward, slipped off the stool, and landed on his feet, staggering. Then he crumpled to the floor. The old man leaned, pulling air with his fingers.

Roder began crawling toward him.

"Leave him alone," I muttered, grabbing his feet. I was getting very irritated. The room felt oppressive and close.

Master Prosper flinched, but kept kneading the air. "Inadequate, creature. He will come to me, and so will you."

"Leave him alone, I said."

No effect. Though I had his legs in the air, Roder was dragging himself along by his fingertips, and he was so strong I couldn't hold him back.

"No! Stop it!" I snapped.

The old man and the young man both winced and laughed.

I dropped Roder's feet and picked up my sword. "Stop her, Yefim!" barked the old man.

Yefim said, "She'll stop me."

I walked past Roder and toward the old man. He stopped making the pulling motions and held his palms up facing me. I could feel my brows pulling together in a scowl. It felt like the heavy air before a thunderstorm.

"Please don't annoy her," said Roder, collapsing onto his arms and panting.

I swung the sword around in the figure-eight motion of the mill, first past my left shoulder and then past my right, pivoting my wrist to make the hissing noises in the air essential for this attack. Its only purpose is to frighten unarmed and unskilled opponents, because anyone with weapon skill knows that wide actions are weak ones. I moved toward the old man, hiss-hiss-step, hiss-hiss-step, hiss-hiss-hiss-hiss-step, yet he still held his hands out, sure he could stop me somehow. I could feel the viscous thickness of the spells he was casting, and had to swallow several times, getting more and more enraged.

I felt the tip of my sword catch and drag, as if it had cut through a thread. A red line appeared across both palms and he flinched, his eyes widening. I continued the mill, making my steps smaller. He pulled his palms back, pulled himself back, and began hitching himself backward up the stairs.

"You—are—making me—kill you," I said between swoops. His foot slipped as he was pushing himself up another step. He lay sprawled on the stairs squinting at my hissing blade. Finally he closed his eyes, awaiting his death. He wasn't going to surrender. Stupid man.

I slapped him in the side of the head with the flat of the blade the way the Sefir Zul did, then kicked him as hard as I could in the easiest available target. He rolled into a ball, his face screwed up in pain, and bumped down several stairs. The other man laughed.

Roder, on all fours, was trying to get up. I grabbed his hand and pulled him to his feet.

"How do you propose to get through a locked door?" said Yefim, perched on the back of a chair and ignoring his master's struggles.

I stood on one foot and kicked like a mule with the other. It didn't budge. I heard something scrambling away on the other side. *Open.*

"The gnat strikes the first blow!" said Yefim, applauding. Master Prosper was still trying to get up.

I adjusted my angle and kicked again. *Open.*

"You are trying to make it angry? The door's enchanted, creature."

I slammed my heel into it a third time, thinking *open open open* until it shuddered free of its lock. Breaking down doors was one part of Zul's training I'd never been good at, that and fighting while hanging from a rope. I pulled Roder out into the big room and shoved the door closed behind me.

By the time we were halfway across, someone was kicking at the door, which seemed to be locked again. Roder was moving more easily, and he managed to scramble out the window after me without hurting himself or making a lot of noise. I crouched outside listening. I heard a distant sound, Yefim laughing, then a yelp of pain in the same voice. Not nice people, those two.

Roder moved farther into the square. "Come on, Malka," he said.

"Roder!" hissed another voice from the front door, and Bielo loped over to join him. "What are you doing? Now you'll really draw attention."

"Their attention was already well drawn," said Roder ruefully. "I'm afraid they saw through me."

"I'm ruined, then," said the innkeeper. "Ruined. We'd better run. They'll treat this as an emergency. They're actually efficient in an emergency." He drew the Monitor along by the arm, but Roder stopped him.

"Malka!" he said, turning.

I began to stand.

Then I began to rise in the air.

Someone was holding me by the collar and lifting me firmly back through the window.

CHAPTER EIGHTEEN

Binding the Blade (*Meeting Teeth,* Taking Edge with Edge)

A droning chant was going on in the background and an argument in the foreground.

"It's an automaton like the other one."

"Nonsense. It's a dybbuk. Smell the necromantic odor it gives off."

"Don't smell too close, or it'll bite your nose off."

General laughter drowning out the chant.

"A very sylph. A lovely sprite from the legends." Young Yefim's voice.

Even more laughter, this time nervous. Many more than two mages were in the room with me this time.

There was some kind of tight bandage wrapped over my mouth, and a dark hood over my head. My hands were bound palm to palm behind my back, wrapped with the same kind of cloth, and my ankles were tied to the rungs of a stool like the one Roder had occupied. They hadn't made the mistake of using magic to capture me this time. Everything that held me captive here was from the material world, and they had used more than the normal restraints when I made the mistake of struggling with all my strength. That didn't mean they weren't using magic on me now. The hood was the least of my oppressions.

It hadn't just been Roder's two interrogators who caught me. They had gotten reinforcements, and it had taken all ten of them to subdue me. I could taste blood in my bound mouth.

"If it were a fetch, we couldn't have tied it up. It's a machine, you idiot. Look at it. Legs and arms and everything, it walks on the ground and breathes with a mouth. It's a material object. Has to be a machine."

The droning stopped and I breathed in a gasp through my nose. "Will you be silent?" said the peevish voice of Master Prosper. "How do you expect me to work if you keep yapping like that?"

"Pardon *me*," said the second voice, the one who thought I was a conjured spirit. "Perhaps you need more help after all."

"You'll just muddy up the works," grumbled Prosper, and my breathing slowed as he started the chant again from the beginning, while the others talked over him, more quietly now. The harsh language, in the mouths of these self-important bureaucrats, lacked the coarse cheer of Bielo's patrons. It crackled and bit, it sanded away at me as I sat muffled and bound in its center. That didn't bother me. What bothered me was what was going on inside me.

Silent and dark like this, frozen in one place, I had to put up with all the changes in me. Yes, I was coming apart at the seams. I wasn't meant to grow this big. But I knew that already, had known it for a long time. There wasn't anything I could do about it, though. If I was given food, I ate, and I grew, and one day I would burst, though I thought I could put it off for a while longer.

The thing that disturbed me more, the thing that indicated more deterioration in me than I'd thought, was a small and simple thing: Bielo and Roder had gotten away, and I was glad, and it was a complicated gladness. They hadn't caught the cat, either, but that pleasure was uncomplicated. Every familiar should have a chance to live free of its master. It was the thought of Roder's freedom, or rather the way I felt about it, and what I'd done about it, that made me upset.

What I had done was deliberately sacrifice my freedom, or at least my possibility of looking innocent, for their freedom. The two mages sent to recapture the two Massims had to be called back hastily to help with me, and I struggled even harder and bespoke them at the top of my voice, when I realized that, so the mages wouldn't be able to leave again. It was just the latest sign of rot, the decay that had started when I apologized to the Sefir Zul. When I did not kill Roder. When I followed Bielo.

"Why is it rocking back and forth like that? Is it trying to escape again? Make it stop."

Hands grabbed my shoulders and tried to hold me in place. I twisted sharply, but that just meant more hands came.

My whole life, until the last few years, I hadn't properly been awake. I'd been no more conscious than my master's dog, and no less, like a very young child with emotions and intelligence but no particular awareness. I came awake on Caliban, but it didn't make me someone else. I was Malka still, just Malka no longer asleep. I had Malka's temper, Malka's cold sharpness, Malka's savage strength. The only thing I added on Caliban was a capacity for self-mockery that helped me pass the time when I was waiting.

This new feeling was different. Very annoying. It was as viscous as syrup, a sour sad feeling like warm vinegar. It was messy and blurred and it smelled as ugly as Bear smelled, before she met me. I regretted that Roder was free. I wanted him here in my place. I was sorry I had done anything to help him. I wished I was out there with him. I was glad he was free. I wanted him to think well of me. It wound around and around.

"Make the creature stay in one place. I can't focus the spell if she moves like that. And stop her making that noise."

Malka the Tragic, the beast whom the gods rewarded and made human but it wouldn't stop barking and scratching itself and it kept piddling in the corners and following strangers home. Or Malka the Buffoon instead, a god condemned to be a small but pompous human.

"Is she crying?"

"I think she's laughing."

"This conjuration is a complete abortion. I will take pleasure in dismembering the ball of dung that made her, whoever the idiot is."

Prosper's chanting voice rose to a creaky height, and they all fell silent, listening. It pushed on me from all sides, swirled around me, swathed me in layers. It was hard enough to breathe through my nose without all that pushing, and I couldn't concentrate.

Stop that.

Exclamations of annoyance. Prosper kept speaking. His spell was sticky and made me want to bite.

Stop it right now.

"What—"

"Great snakes, I never—"

STOP that.

"How can it bespeak with its mouth sealed?"

"Well, it's doing it," a grim rejoinder.

"Yes, I'd noticed, thank you for pointing that out."

"I'll put a protection shield up for us, then."

"You? You couldn't shield against a raindrop. I'll do it."

These mages couldn't open their mouths without arguing.

After that, they didn't notice anything I said. Prosper's voice got louder and more insistent. I couldn't make out any words, but it sounded as if he were repeating himself. Yes, he was repeating himself, and now he did it again, with even more volume, and his spell pushed and pushed at me, all over. It was very annoying, and I was tempted to push back.

Instead, I pulled. I sucked the spell in like a noodle.

He screamed.

So did I, or rather I squeaked through my nose. It had been just enough magic to make me grow again, and the bandages around my head and hands dug in sharply. So did my armor.

"Master? Master?" said worried voices, and there was scuffling.

"Is he dead?"

"No, worse luck," said the voice of the one who thought I was a conjured spirit. "Help me prop him up. He's breathing."

They applied damp rags and ice to Prosper, waved something under his nose, and babbled healing spells. They seemed far more interested in their ongoing arguments than in me. It gave me thought. I couldn't bespeak them directly with their shield up, and even if I could I couldn't get them to free me—I could never make people do anything completely against their will—but maybe I could get them to pay attention to something besides me.

I took a breath in through my nose, and let it out slowly. Gently now, let it seep out like water into a dry sponge. *There are more important things to worry about.*

"Well, this is all Council's fault anyway, if you ask me," said one of the more earnest voices. "They haven't been doing their job."

That apparently woke Prosper up, for he began to argue in a thin petulant voice that Council couldn't possibly have any effect on anything whatsoever because its members were charlatans, weaklings, libertines, and completely irrelevant. Council was beside the point. One of the others agreed that the point was to find out whether the captive was an automaton or a succubus.

Far more important things to worry about. Gently, gently. Lord, the bandage hurt.

The others laughed at him. "Don't be petty," said one.

I'll keep.

"The creature will keep," said Prosper grumpily, and I could hear him getting to his feet and swearing at the mages who were trying to help him up. "We need to be more systematic about this. The spells that protect this monster are strong. If we want to get inside it and find what it's made of, we have to plan better. And besides—"

Far more important things.

"—there are other more important things going on. There have been so many disturbances lately. Things falling out of the sky. Renegade mages seducing council members. Herb-wives getting mixed up with everything. Exploding houses. Strangers speaking nonsense. Ghosts. This creature is only a symptom. We need to get at the source . . ."

But they didn't leave the room. Instead, they sent out one of their number to bring more supplies. From the sounds, they were setting up some kind of circle on the other side of the room, wrangling and bickering, casting side spells whose overflow made me itch and wriggle. One of the side spells was particularly nasty.

"I caught that!" said one of them abruptly, and there was a frozen silence.

"My pardon," said Yefim politely.

The first voice said, "If you attempt to spell-afflict me again

I will permanently remove the skin on your buttocks and set you to spinning on them."

"But of course. My apologies," said Yefim. "Won't happen." The chatter and cursing rose again as if this were normal conversation. It probably was.

This was the kind of world my master wanted, a world where witches ran everything, where your influence depended on how good you were at persuading magic to do what you want. Where the government was an uneasy truce between individuals with power who were temporarily agreeing not to flay one another alive, and where people without power undoubtedly had no say in the matter. My little master would fit right in.

"Now," said Master Prosper finally. "We are agreed? The purpose is to find the origin of all the recent disturbances?"

"Not all, surely," objected another. "Some of it must be the usual stuff."

"All right, all right. This creature, then? And the falling house, and the mechanical man."

"The pale ghost."

"And the naked brown woman talking nonsense!"

"All those people talking nonsense. And slipping their containment spell."

They were Pegeen and the rest of Roder's crew. And who was the pale ghost? Then I remembered the thing that had been inside Tobiah, the hand inside the puppet. It must still be running around.

"We begin," said Prosper formally, and then spoiled it by saying, "You call this a seeing-vessel?" but eventually they all got down to business. It was a long chant. I concentrated on breathing through my nose. They were pushing on me hard. At the same time, though, they were creating a concentration of magic as big as an engine right there in the room. It was way too big for what they were trying to do, but I supposed they didn't know it. Even though I couldn't see anything, I could feel the warmth of the magic they were drawing to them with their incantation. It was like sitting at a fire.

My gag got tighter. The bands around my ankles and hands pulled harder.

"Something is messing this up," a peevish voice complained, interrupting the chant.

"Probably your incompetence," and they were all on their feet shouting at one another. Two of them, from the shouts, were trying to hit each other.

The captive is the problem. Remove the captive.

"It's the monster," said Prosper dryly, when the wranglers had been separated. "She's disturbing the flow. Remove her."

They carried me, stool and all, into another room and shut the door.

I was alone in the room, only the small sound of my breathing to accompany me. Now that I was by myself, I realized that to be tied up alone with my thoughts and the pain of my bonds wasn't necessarily the best alternative I could have chosen. I breathed for a long time, sometimes rocking back and forth, sometimes laughing through my nose.

Something warm landed in my lap and I nearly fell off the stool.

"Miiiiiiine," said Bear's comfortable voice, and she stood kneading my thighs with her paws.

Yours, small spirit, I agreed, and laughed, and laughed again.

What amused me was I found her presence consoling. I cared that somebody cared for me, even if she loved me because I was keeping her alive with my overflow. Yes, I was definitely falling apart. It had come to this. Malka, the Savage So Solitary in Splendor, taking comfort from a mangy artificial cat. Did humans feel this way all the time? I couldn't bear the thought. Why didn't they all just kill themselves and be done with it?

"Mine," she murmured, turned around, and lay down with her back against my belly.

CHAPTER NINETEEN

Broken Time (*Carmichael Bah,* Change in Tempo Used to Fool Opponent)

The cat jumped out of my lap, a sudden jolt.

"Poor thing. Look what they did to her."

It wasn't a voice I'd expected to hear. Cully's.

Another voice, belonging to Fergus, annoyed. "Hold off. I have to undo the window wards."

"How could they do that to the poor little monkey?"

I am not a monkey.

"Stop being sentimental, Cully, or she'll hurt you again." Roder. They'd found him, then.

"You're all being too sentimental, if you ask me," said Electra bitterly. "Be quiet or the locals will come running. I can only muffle so much sound."

"Okay, you're in." Sounds of scrambling. Hands on my arms. The hood lifting off. Seven intent faces, and Cully trying to undo the bandage.

Idiot.

"Pick her up the way she is and let's get out of here. We can untie her later," said Roder calmly. I knew I could count on him.

Fergus took my feet and Cully went around behind me to lift me by the shoulders, and they loaded me and my stool out of the window to Electra and Pegeen, who were waiting outside, both looking entirely recovered and far more clothed than when I last saw them. The cat was washing herself in the middle of the square.

"Not here, either," Roder said impatiently, righting me when Electra and Pegeen tried to lay me down outside to undo me. "Can't you see she's got yards of the stuff around her? We'd be half an hour unwinding her here. Pegeen, can you cover our tracks?" Pegeen, pushing her glasses up her nose, nodded absentmindedly. She was wearing somebody's trousers, far too big for her, and a woven shirt that made her look like a stick.

"The poor thing is suffocating like that," objected Cully.

"Are you, Malka?"

I continue to breathe.

"Ouch. Fine, then," said Roder, and there were no more objections.

We were not returning to Bielo's tavern, but making our way through side streets nearer the top of the city-hill, where all the elaborate houses were. Bielo led the way, the set of his shoulders conveying how very frivolous and tedious it was of us to need his help.

"Here, I think. Yes, here," he said, stopping. "It was owned by a mage who died just last year, and his neighbors have been gone for decades."

The house didn't look abandoned. It was made of a sunny sandstone in chalky pastels of yellow and a soft, comfortable rose. Its lines were sturdy and worn, and the quiet light illuminating its facade seemed to come from everywhere and nowhere.

Fergus put down the bag he was carrying, kneeled, and put his forehead against the stone door. His parrot waddled importantly back and forth from shoulder to shoulder. Something clicked.

The door swung open a crack and a dusty smell of pollen washed over us. There was birdsong, and even more glowing light.

Inside, there was the sound of running water. Waxed wood was warm beneath my bare feet as Roder undid the tight yards of fabric around my wrists. My hands, when I held them up to look at them, were creased and blue and without feeling. It was remarkable how human I was getting. I even had blood circulation to be impaired now.

Roder untucked the end of my gag and undid it by pulling it upward so it spiraled around my head. Everyone else except for Bielo was off exploring the house. Bielo sat on a wooden bench in the front room watching us.

"She doesn't find you attractive, you know, not in the usual way," the innkeeper said as Roder neared the end of the gag.

"Oh, I know," answered Roder with that sweet smile as he took the last of it off.

"Shtop zhat," I said, and had to stop myself because there was lint all over my tongue. This wouldn't do. It wouldn't do at all. I had to get out of this. Now I was free of the mages, I could get away on my own.

"Thank you, Malka, for rescuing me," answered Roder gravely, kissed my hand, and went into the other room.

Bielo didn't move from the bench.

You have better things to do with your time.

He looked blank for a moment, then said, "Won't wash. What is it you want to do that I can't watch?"

"I want to think."

He still didn't move.

"Alone."

"I don't agree," he said amiably. "From the condition of your face, it looks like you spent the last three hours thinking alone. If you're going to leave, you at least have to let Roder know. He went to great lengths to get you out. Now don't get all mad at me."

My sword wasn't in its scabbard. I whirled around, but it was nowhere in the room.

"The big fellow brought your scimitar along. It's in the other room," said Bielo. "You won't kill me, though. Roder said. You look like a goblin when you're angry, did you know that?"

I screamed at him.

"Malka," Roder said from the doorway, the others crowding behind.

"She wants to run away," said Bielo, in a complacent tattling tone.

"Let her," said Roder, crossing his arms and leaning against the jamb. "Cully, give her the sword."

Bielo glared at him in astonishment. Cully gave him a look of outrage too, but handed the weapon over.

"You want something to eat before you go?" Roder inquired. "Fergus stole quite a selection from the open-air market. There are some cheeses in here that smell positively ethereal."

"I am not a feral cat to be tempted with food," I said. "I am not a horse to be broken. I am not a monkey to be trained."

"No," agreed the Massim. The eyes were calm. "You are a great and powerful being. A noble hero. A mighty warrior."

I couldn't help it. I laughed. "Malka the Mighty," I agreed, and stamped my foot. Then I walked out of the front door of the house and stood in the lane outside, making a sort of humming noise that I couldn't stop making.

Nobody came out of the door after me. Nobody came down the road. I was all by myself. If I wanted to, I could walk away right now.

I stamped my foot again. A small foot. A small noise. I whirled.

"Aaaaaaaaaaah!" I shouted at the house.

Roder opened the door. "Yes?"

"I could blow up the world," I said. "I could kill you with a word. You do not know what I am. What is wrong with you?"

"I've never met anybody like you before," he said, with simple wonder.

"Aaaaaaah!" I shouted again, shaking my head back and forth, feeling like a wounded bear and undoubtedly looking like an annoyed parakeet.

"I'm sorry," he said. "I'm making it difficult. Go ahead and leave. I'll understand. Could you tell me something before you go?"

"What?" I growled, not sure I wanted him telling me to leave.

That sweet smile, and the river-colored eyes neither sad nor bored, and with no pity in them for me. "Do you like me? Because I like you, very much. Please stay. It would make me happy."

"Stop that."

"No. I want you to stay. I'll do whatever it takes."

He was leaning against the doorjamb again, his arms folded. He probably knew he looked good standing like that. I waited for him to go back inside. That was the next thing he'd do, pretend I was completely free, that he wasn't manipulating me.

He didn't go.

"Besides, Enforcement will undoubtedly find me eventually, and if they find me they'll go looking for you."

And if they found me, so would my master.

"I'm dangerous to you. To everyone," I said, feeling that I had already lost.

"I've marooned myself and blown up my engine on a low-tech renegade non-Web world. I've made the local administration very angry with me and very curious about my inner workings. There's a Web-wide government coup going on in my absence which I'm trying to stop single-handed. I've irritated Enforcement enough that they spent years setting you and your young friend up as my assassins and now they've got half their ships out trying to kill me. Meanwhile I'm trying to rescue an entire planet-load of Mennenkalt refugees, save the Web, and keep my crew alive. I'm more dangerous to myself than you could ever be."

He reached out his palms, but not as if he expected me to take them. It was more like the display of a sword-fight referee, showing he had no concealed weapons himself.

I stared at him.

The cat's heart-shaped face appeared between his legs, its whiskers brushing against his trousers. She rubbed her small head against him, marking him as her property, then sat down to give herself a thorough washing as if she had just had a hearty meal. Three houses down, I heard a door open and shut.

The android stood straight, stepped out of the door, making the cat jump away in annoyance, and he took my off hand, ignoring the half-raised sword and drawing me back into the house. "Come on back," he said. "You can always change your mind later."

I went with him. It was easier than standing in the street fighting with myself.

CHAPTER TWENTY

Body Parry (*Corps-à-Corps,*
The Strategic Tackle)

The cheese was indeed very good, as was the thick-seeded rosemary-flavored bread Fergus had stolen to accompany it, and the tart crunchy pears. I sat cross-legged, feeling like a newly hatched chick, on a ledge at one end of a large back room while the others are more or less in the middle, sorting themselves into a chart of social dynamics.

The just-hatched feeling was because they'd had to cut me out of my armor before I could eat. It lay in a pile in the front room, stretched and sliced and torn, no longer usable for anything. There was no hope for it; I had grown so much I couldn't bend my elbows or knees while I was wearing the stuff. Roder had drawn me back into the house like a child's pull-toy, and when he saw how much I was hobbling he made me lie down on the floor right there so he could get it off. Bielo had a pocket-knife, so he busily took over, complaining all the while, but he somehow managed not to cut the fabric of my black shirt and skins underneath while he ripped and muttered. Roder didn't bother to watch. He went into the other room.

"Are you older or younger than Roder?" I asked Bielo suddenly while he was slitting my left sleeve.

"Ha. Why do you ask? Because I didn't play martyr when I got stuck on this planet?"

"No."

"It's none of your business."

"Well, then, why do people like you and Roder so much? What did they put in the Massim to make you that way? Because the standard model was just an all-purpose diplomat."

"Hm. You know some interesting things." He was working

136

the tip of the knife millimeter by millimeter over the crown of my shoulder, where the leather was stretched so tight my flesh bulged out through the opening he was making. I didn't think he was going to answer, but when he rounded the point he started talking again.

"You familiar with any cults?"

"Like the Mennenkalts?"

"No, that's an established religion. Anything that survives its prophet usually hangs together around its articles of faith, not because of the personality of its leader."

"Oh. Then the Disciples of the Light. And Mahwah Brethren, and the Blessed Flood."

"Right. Tell me about Brother Jonah of the Disciples."

I tried to remember. I'd seen pictures. "Blue eyes. Sort of dirty hair, medium long, and he had a deep voice."

"No, not his coloring or his hygiene. What impression did he give?"

"I don't know. Grimy and pompous. I never could figure out his appeal."

"Ah." Bielo tipped my head back and neatly slit the collar open, then began working his way down the other sleeve. I took a breath. My abdomen was still encased, but my throat was free. "I'll tell you. He gave an impression of inner certainty, of complete attention, and of calm. Also he had a great deal of physical presence, and he exuded sexual power."

"If you say so." Jonah was very dirty indeed, and he lived in a truck in a junkyard and I could never understand why his young followers believed anything he said.

"Well, then, Mahwah Brethren. Tell me about Mahwah Jebum."

I couldn't shrug. I wasn't following this line at all. "Dark skin. Sun goggles. Broad shoulders. Wore a hat all the time."

"You're missing the point. Certainty, attention, calm, presence, and sex. Doesn't hurt if they have brooding anger, too, like Mahwah did."

"Mahwah? Sex?" The man had looked like a tree trunk, thick and stiff. His people all wore hats and goggles too and burned themselves with acid under their tan-colored tunics.

"Yes, Mahwah. He exuded it. Though I heard he was limp as a dumpling when it came down to the actual rough-bump. How about the Blessed Flood—Old Eoghan."

"Skinny man with pop eyes who looked like his Adam's apple was about to leap through the top of his head. Sexy as a celery stick."

"You're impossible," said Bielo, reaching the wrist. I took a deep breath and felt my shoulders rise above the ragged front. He stripped the remains of the jacket off and threw them to one side, then started at my right ankle, slitting neatly up toward my knee. "A ship's crew has to be made of witches, or the boat won't go, right? And a Monitor ship can't be crewed by Polytechnic graduates, so they have to be free witches. Free witches are dangerous and they want more than anything to get away. Can you see why the Monitor has to be very charismatic? When they designed the Monitor Massims, they threw in a dash of cult-leader personality. Certainty, attention, calm, presence, and sex. Stop laughing, I'm holding a knife to your kneecap."

"And humans get fooled by that?"

He gave me a puzzled look and kept cutting. "You try separating a Monitor's crew from their Monitor. In fact, the first run of Massims was so attractive they toned the later ones down. Caused too many troubles. Crushes, jealousy, suicides."

That answered my first question. "Then you're younger than Roder."

He pursed up his mouth and kept cutting up the casing over my thigh, efficiently sliding the point a centimeter forward and then ripping upward. Then he smiled.

"I'm not going to tell you," he said, and cut through my waistband to free one leg. "I'll just tell you they took out some of the need for power and control the earlier ones had when they toned the later ones down." Then he cut the other leg of my trousers off without saying any more.

When I went into the other room to get something to eat, I could see it laid out just as Bielo had said. Roder, though he sat silent against a wall separate from the others, was the center of the room's energy. They weren't looking at him, though. Fergust and Cully sat together to one side of him, not facing him,

Fergus eating bread and leaning against the Calypsan's knee where the priest sat in his chair. The parrot was on the back of the chair. Pegeen and Octavian were sitting facing each other on the other side of him, and Octavian had his feet propped on the chair's seat either side of Pegeen's skinny thighs. Electra was against the opposite wall with her small furry familiar in her lap, alternately stroking and squeezing it, her head bent down. But even though they weren't looking at him, they had arranged themselves so he could see exactly what they were doing, as if they were children being good for Father Solstice.

I grabbed some cheese and bread and climbed into the ledge at the back of the room, and became part of the tableau: Malka the Household God, small, hot, savage, and ignored on the family altar. Roder glanced at me. I scowled at him. When I looked away, Electra was clutching her small animal and glaring at me herself.

Crushes, jealousy, suicides.

"I have to go back," said Bielo from the doorway. "I've done more than I said I would. I need to go home and get ready for the morning." I heard the front door closing quietly.

"Sleep, people, sleep," Roder said, leaning forward and rubbing his eyes. Pegeen was already leaning back with a piece of fruit in one dark hand, her eyes closed, and her opinionated mouth slack. Octavian put a toe in her belly and she snorted without opening her eyes. Cully and Fergus were already on their way up the stairs, Cully's arm slung across the engineer's shoulder, his beads clutched in the other hand. There must be beds up there.

I didn't move, myself. The ledge was warm and high off the ground and just because I had come back inside didn't mean I was one of Roder's tame dogs. But Electra didn't move, either. Nor did Roder.

"Go to bed," he said to her.

She gave her small animal a squeeze and it squeaked and struggled. She let it get out of her hands and then grabbed it by the tail as it scrabbled to get away. It squeaked again. Bear was watching it intently, her tail trembling at the tip.

"Let it go," I said.

The woman grabbed it around the middle instead, and shoved it head down into a pouch at her waist, not looking at me. The pouch squeaked and convulsed. She stood up too abruptly and left. I could hear her stamping up the stairs.

Roder stood up and came over to my ledge, leaning on it with both arms and looking up at me. "You say you're not a witch. The way you grow—you're not even human, are you, Malka?" he said. "You're a creature of magic yourself."

"Let it go," I said again. *Let it go let it go let it go.* I wouldn't explain anything to him.

He made that open-palm gesture again. "I have no pouch to put you in." He laid one of the palms down on my ankle. Warm and dry and light, as impersonal as ever. Something pale seemed to move outside in the street, but when I looked up it was gone.

"Go away," I told him, "I'd kill you." I opened my mouth wide, and breathed on him. When the heat of my breath hit him, he pulled his face back a half a centimeter, shocked. He got the point, all right.

"No wonder you wouldn't let me take your temperature," he said. "You could boil an egg in that mouth." He lifted his hand from me. "I went for a swim in the hot springs at Ahulani once," he told me gravely. "Very refreshing."

Then he went away too.

Certainty, attention, calm, presence, and never-you-mind, and the hot springs at Ahulani were boiling mud the natives used to cook entire cows. He was like a thoroughly civilized Sefir Zul, and about as dangerous to me as Zul was. Yes, I had become too human.

CHAPTER TWENTY-ONE

Indirect Attack
(*Huong's Corkscrew,* Striking the Unexpected Target)

I wandered into the front room, rubbing my eyes. It was mid-morning, and everyone was up again, most looking the worse for their sleep. Electra's elaborate hairdo wasn't meant to be slept upon, and the knot on the back of her head had partly unraveled. Her oval face, though smooth as ever, looked even more offended. Cully's face was puffy, and his wide-set eyes were small as those of a blinking child. Pegeen had gray scuffs on her brown skin, and thin-skinned Fergus looked crumpled up and unfolded like a piece of salvaged wastepaper. Only Octavian and the cat seemed unaffected, both of them grooming themselves, though Octavian seemed to be listening to something only he could hear, his eyes closed while he combed his long black hair and bound it neatly up.

They were trying to find magic so they could make a new engine.

"Any concentration of magic at all," said Roder, standing next to a low fountain and looking out the front window. A bird flew through the room, a swift flash of bright blue, but he ignored it.

"No, it has to be at least a certain size," said Octavian doggedly, not opening his eyes, and from the way Roder hunched his shoulders forward I realized Octavian was working and I'd come into an ongoing argument.

"I told you, we can merge them if they're not big enough."

"I'm not going to even *try* to talk to an engine with a split personality," said Octavian.

"Couldn't drive it," agreed Fergus.

Roder must be trying to make his own engine.

"Magic is not made up of personalities! You're anthropomorphizing," the android said to the window.

"Look who's talking," said Pegeen. "Bet you'd be plenty cranky if we said you didn't have a personality because you're manufactured."

Roder blew his breath out.

Octavian opened his eyes and tied the final knot in his ribbon. "It's beside the point, anyway. Even if you put all the magic from all the spells on all these houses together, you still wouldn't have enough to translate a mouse. I have to look farther away." He stretched himself out on the floor and folded his hands on his chest, like a decorative corpse.

"Shut up, Malka," said Octavian. "Like trying to thread beads in a hurricane." I hadn't said anything. Hadn't *said* anything either.

Roder kept looking out the window.

"Mages are looking for us," Octavian commented idly a little while later. "All-points bulletin about a mechanical man, a succubus, several assorted babbling idiots, and a ghost."

"We're the babbling idiots," said Pegeen. "We speak a foreign language, and they only know their own. Malka's the succubus. Roder's the windup toy."

"What's the ghost?" said Cully.

Something knocked on the door and everybody froze. Roder, unperturbed, had already seen the visitor coming and opened the door. Bielo walked in.

"You put me out of business," he said bitterly. "I didn't even make it inside; they'd boarded me up and plastered a sign on the door. Harboring fugitives. Suspicion of unauthorized conjuring. You put me out of business and out on the street. I told you. You can count on them to be inefficient as long as you don't get their attention, but you got their attention."

Roder shut the door behind him and went back to the window.

"And you don't care, either, do you?"

Roder shrugged, as if a shrug were a complete explanation. Maybe it was, because Bielo didn't seem to have anything more to say. He looked down at the witch on the floor.

"There's a big enough concentration of magic down that way,' said Octavian, pointing from his prone position. Bielo stared the way he was pointing, which was near the corner of the back wall.

"He's looking for something we can use for an engine," said Roder.

"If he's looking the direction I think, that's the Beast and it's more likely to use *you*," said Bielo.

"Beast?"

"A local witch thing. An initiation ordeal, a spell sealed in a building. Mages go to the Beast when they're finished learning to be mages. All they have to do is walk through the building. They live, they pass. They die, they fail. You won't be able to do anything with it. It's hundreds of years old and set in its ways."

"We can try," said Roder. "It's big enough."

"You can't reuse a ready-made spell for an engine," I said. "Bielo's right. It won't work."

You could hear the sound of every eye in the room rolling.

"An opinion for every occasion," said Electra and flinched, though I hadn't actually done anything.

Roder said from the window, "Why not, Malka? No, I have my reasons for asking," he said mildly in answer to the expressions. "Why not, Malka?"

"You think magic is just . . . stuff. Clay."

"Well, yes, it is just stuff. Psicleons. Quasi-sentient, infinitely malleable, mentoid, nonbaryonic pseudomatter," said Fergus, meaning "what's your point."

"Stuff. Stuff that sort of thinks and you can make it do whatever you want if you just use the right words," I said. "That's what humans believe."

"And it isn't?" said Cully, bewildered.

Fergus said, closing his eyes, "No, all human beings don't think magic is just stuff. The Mennenkalts think magic is god. The Terps think it's the devil, the Hom Bulos refer to it as RGWG the Unnamable, and the Shoemaker Cabal call it life's heartblood and sacrifice chickens to it. The Polytechnic teaches that it's a virtual potentiality of a multidimensional partially collapsed universe. The Enforcement tech people think it's raw mathematical information. All right? Does that cover it? So?"

I was silent.

Roder leaned his elbows on the sill behind him.

I said to him, only to him, "A Web engine isn't a place or a thing. It's a condition. It contains its ship, not the other way around."

"What?" said Electra. "Roder—"

"Spatial inversion," said Fergus. "Well, yeah, of course, it involves a twist in space. The engine in a ship is inside out and bigger than its ship. Like ship scenery."

I nodded. He was completely wrong but in a useful way.

"I have no idea what you're all talking about," said Electra.

"You're saying we'd have to start from scratch?" said Roder. "None of my crew is powerful enough to make an engine from scratch, Malka."

I closed my mouth suddenly. What was I getting myself into? I wouldn't say any more. *Forget it.* The tides rose inside me, slowly, and subsided. Everybody in the room sat staring into space, quiet and content.

Roder said, "What were we talking about? Oh, yes, are there any of the local witches who could build an engine, Bielo? I don't need a big one."

Bielo looked down at his hands. "There's some mages who could, but no one who would. They're a provincial lot, don't know the stars are suns and don't care, and translation isn't something they're curious about. There's one of the mages who used to talk about the idea, but they all made fun of him. He's one who could make you an engine, too, very powerful witch, but he's out of town and I don't know when he'll be back, or even if he'll be back. Or you could scout around for a renegade, but they're even less trustworthy than the local bunch of bureaucrats."

"I need an engine," Roder repeated. "Find me someone who can build an engine and I'll take care of the persuading. Meanwhile we have to try everything we can. We'll go look at this Beast. Octavian and Fergus, you come with me." He opened the door and went out.

Bielo sighed.

"You're going with him, of course?" said Electra behind where I stood watching them.

"He didn't ask me," I said.

"I'm not going to try to stop you."

Pegeen said wearily, "Electra. Get over it."

Electra left the room smoothly, the effect marred only by the loops of hair sticking out behind.

"Not your fault, child," said Pegeen steadily. "Akamai's death upset her more than most."

"Upset's a good word," agreed Cully. "Like upsetting a stack of dishes. She was so sure she was next in line."

"Talk to your beads, priest," said Pegeen coldly, and Cully didn't say anything. It reminded me of the students in the Sefir Zul's school, the sideways glances, the disdainful expressions when you complimented the form of someone who was out of the room. "Next in line," indeed, like being next in line for one of Zul's lessons. A dubious honor.

The Sefir Zul, in his own way, was very much like the people Bielo had been talking about. Certainty, attention, calm, presence, a well-exercised capacity for anger, and heaven knows what the other female students saw—or smelled—in him because I certainly didn't.

Next in line.

I slipped out the door and saw the others up ahead. Roder, his shoulders relaxed, walked like a king with Octavian and Fergus attending him two steps behind. I followed farther back, thinking unuseful thoughts.

The others, when I caught up with them, were staring at a shabby stone building with an unfinished wooden door at the front and another at the back, standing alone on a hill overlooking the river. It looked abandoned, though there was a worn path leading up to the door from a gate in the stone wall surrounding it. I could smell the magic, warm and aromatic.

"Are you sure?" asked Roder, and Octavian nodded, not taking his eyes off the building.

"Big as the Ong's Hat Cybernal," the boy said. "Big as Malka."

"Too big," said Fergus, taking the second statement for a lame joke and looking worried.

"Be quiet, I'm trying to talk to it." Octavian sank down into a cross-legged squat and covered his eyes with his hands.

The morning wind rolled up from the harbor, carrying the sulfur reek of well-aged mud. A seagull angled overhead. The parrot on Fergus' shoulder bobbed its head at it and shifted from foot to foot. Out here, near the river harbor, you could see the way the city was built on the gently curved sides of a small, low mountain that dangled its feet in the water. You could see the weathered ranks of the lower-level buildings break into gaudy splendor like an orchid budding from tree bark about three-quarters of the way up the hill, and from here you couldn't see that the beautiful houses were, most of them, empty.

"Hst! Down!" said Roder, and I was flat on my belly.

A horseman came through the gate, a body with bound hands slung across his horse's withers in front of him. The rider was in grubby white robes, had a long white beard and a hooked nose. Another rider followed him, a young man.

The riders didn't see us. The old man stopped before the door of the building, and the young man dismounted and ran forward to help him slide his captive off the horse. Their prisoner seemed to be awake, though not completely. He staggered as they set him on his feet, and seemed to be asking something of the air. The younger man shoved him toward the door, opened it, and pushed the captive inside. They followed after him.

"A captured renegade," said Bielo.

Roder said to him, "They have to take the final exam whether they went through the training or not? Those are strict standards."

Bielo nodded, his face sideways on the ground.

Octavian hadn't moved from his sitting position, even though the rest of us were lying down. Now his shoulders were shaking.

"Whoa," he said, opening his eyes in surprise. "Waking up now. It's waking up. Watch out . . . Hello."

The building hadn't moved. The same spicy smell of magic came from it. Octavian, however, was watching it with complete surprise.

"Ow. No. No, I'm not. Ow," he said. Then there was a long, long pause. Abruptly he gave a long groan and began to get up. Fergus grabbed his ankle as he went past. Octavian looked down at him, said, "I know what I'm doing," shook it off, and kept going toward the shabby building.

"I think it's got him in its net," said Fergus. "They threw the native in and it started and it's taking Octavian too."

Roder went after him. He grabbed Octavian's shoulder and turned him around. They were arguing.

The front door of the building opened, and a startled face looked out. There was a shout.

Octavian turned as if to keep going, and Roder ducked down and stood up again with the boy over his shoulder. Another shout came, and the first face was joined by a second.

"Hup, let's go," said Roder, jogging past us.

"Oh-for-hea-ven's-sake-put-me-down," said Octavian in syllables jerked out by his bouncing.

"Not likely." They were pulling ahead, away from Fergus and me, and Fergus began to run in earnest. Bielo could run just as fast as Roder and was even with them. I could hear Octavian still arguing, but within a block I couldn't make out the words. I might have grown in the last few days, but I was still shorter than most humans and no stronger, and I couldn't keep up.

Someone behind me shouted again, and when I turned around the two locals were running after me. I took the first left turn, still plugging away. I heard their voices behind me, and I darted between two houses, then ran back the way I had come along a narrow alleyway. I turned right and chugged back down toward the house of the local Beast, glancing to one side to see my two pursuers heading away from me down the first street I'd taken. Intentionally or not, I'd thrown them off the trail of the others as well.

You can catch me if you just keep going, I said. Then I turned off and headed zigzag fashion toward my goal, thinking as I encountered other people, *not worth noticing, not worth noticing.* Nobody was dressed like me, though my black shirt and skins would have passed on a hundred worlds. The people wore yards and yards of fabric. The women wore long full skirts, the men trousers, full-sleeved shirts, and tunics. The children wore loose garments down to their knees and their hair was shorter than mine.

It was the first time I'd been alone since I ran from the Enforcer at Zul's. I liked being alone. Up until a few years before, I was always alone, because no one ever noticed me when I was small. If they saw me at all, I was a shadow just at the edge of eyesight. Just like the pale shadow I kept seeing out of the corner of my eye now.

I turned around and caught it slipping away. Skinny legs, skinny arms, and it turned steady blue eyes back toward me as it ran. It was the pale thing that had been inside Tobiah.

I still wasn't alone.

CHAPTER TWENTY-TWO

Passé (*Hayakutake*, Attack That Passes without Striking the Opponent)

"The Beast wants to talk to me, and I want to talk to it," said Octavian doggedly. He was standing with his arms folded. Pegeen, still as a judge, sat on a bench watching him.

"That may be true, but can't you put it off until this is over?" Roder said patiently. "We can't risk exposing ourselves to the locals anymore. They're already looking for us."

When I came in the door, it seemed nobody had noticed I wasn't there. Nobody paid attention now I *was* there.

"I speak directly to magic," said Octavian, slowly and clearly. "It speaks directly to me. It's always saying crazy things to me and trying to get me to do things, because magic is insane. Every Cybernal and every engine in the Web is completely crazy because they're under so much pressure. This one is not insane. I know, because I am talking with it right now. It just wants to talk with me."

"If you're talking with it now, why do you have to go into that building?" asked Pegeen.

"It's made so you have to be inside it to talk properly. That's what it does when it examines witches. They go inside it."

"Why you? What's special about you?"

"I talk back to magic. It doesn't meet many people who can talk back."

"You are chosen because you are special. Only you. You go to a strange world, stop by the local temple, and the god speaks to only you," said Roder gently.

"It's not a fantasy!"

149

"No. It's a trap. It's a swindle."

"You would know, wouldn't you?" said Octavian.

Roder didn't say anything, just watched him with those eyes.

"I want to talk to it," repeated Octavian, not looking at him.

"Pegeen, would you take him upstairs and keep him safe until he gets a little more reasonable?" asked Roder.

"You mean until he agrees with you?" she said.

"I mean until he can see my side at all."

"Oh. In that case, yes."

I listened to their footsteps creaking on the wooden stairs, and the quiet thumps upstairs as they moved about. The sunny little house didn't seem so sunny in the daytime, though a peach-colored bird perched on a high molding was carefully running its beak through its feathers. The sound of trickling water still came from somewhere else in the house, but I found it irritating rather than soothing. It was my opinion Octavian knew what he was talking about. If the Beast thing was conscious and it had lived a long time inside that house, it was extremely bored.

"I've never heard of that happening before," said Bielo. "The Beast just waits for its victims, generally. Have you considered—"

"The boy was raised to be easily led," Roder replied. "He's a human plaything."

"Doesn't look that easy to me."

"Malka was right. We're going to have to make an engine ourselves. And we can't." He paused. "Thought maybe you were intending to leave us, when you didn't choose to come back with us," said Roder to me, the first time he'd looked at me since I came in the front door panting.

Cully raised his eyes from his beads. Electra was already watching me. "Whoo," commented Fergus, the only person in the room who wasn't staring at me, but only because he was looking at the ceiling. "St. Stephen's perforated undershirt."

It took me off guard. I was not a member of Roder's crew. I was not his possession. He couldn't tell me what to do. I wasn't going to explain about how short I was and how hard it was to run fast. Besides, he had said I could leave if I felt like it.

"Child, you really should have stayed with the group," agreed

Electra. "You could have gotten lost." She had repaired her hairdo since we went out. She looked smooth, sleek, perfect, and utterly forlorn, and she was petting her small furry familiar with short rapid strokes. Its blinking eyes looked pinker than usual.

Leave me alone.

Roder winced, but Electra, still staring at me, stroked her familiar so hard it whined. She frowned at it and gave it a shake. It closed its eyes.

"Let it go."

"What?"

"Let go of your familiar. You're hurting it."

"It's not even a real animal, child," she said. "I made it myself. I can do what I want with it."

"It made itself. You asked it, and it made itself. It does you a favor by existing. Now let go of it."

She squeezed the small furry thing harder, maybe not deliberately, and the animal shrieked. So I jumped on her.

Roder pried my hands off her while Bielo dealt with her. Roder carried me by my arms up the stairs, ignoring my heels on his thighs and the attempts I was making to bite him. Once we were inside the upstairs room and the door was closed, I backed against the far wall and glared at him.

I showed my teeth.

He shrugged. "So you're not human. I'm not human either."

I opened my mouth to scream at him and closed it again.

"We're going to have to make this up as we go along," he said. He had been leaning with his back against the door waiting for me to finish, and now he straightened and moved forward, the door opening a crack behind him as he released the pressure.

"You're the one making things up," I said fiercely, and didn't know what to do with my hands, so I put them behind my back. My sword was somewhere downstairs on the floor. He took another step forward, and I backed up until I was up against the far wall. The window next to me was open, and I briefly thought about jumping through it and climbing down the tree outside.

"Well, if I'm making things up, then once upon a time there was an android and he met a fallen angel . . ." he said, shrugged again, and kneeled in front of me.

"Fallen angel my elbow. Fallen squirrel from a tree," I said. He didn't smile, just stayed there looking up at me, the sun from the window slanting across his face so that his eyes shone.

I had to lean down just a little bit to kiss his mouth, which I did eventually, very carefully. His skin was very dry, and nearly as warm as mine. I brushed my lips against his, and pulled my head away to consider the encounter. He had his hands behind his back, too, I saw.

He kneeled looking at me for what seemed far too long, so eventually I kissed him again, more firmly. Nothing broke. He didn't grab me or push at me. He just kissed me back, and when I parted my lips he did too, and turned his head slightly.

I wasn't giving him any steam burns. I was getting a crick in my neck, though. I didn't understand any of this. I never had. When I was little, it was irrelevant to me how humans justified their instincts to themselves, and when I got bigger, it was of no interest.

My master's pleasures almost made more sense to me. There was a grand fascination to the idea of death and ending, much more extraordinary than the mechanics involved in starting new life.

Kissing was better than it looked, though, I was finding. *Yes.* That was because he kissed me only when I wanted him to. It was frightening to have anyone paying such complete attention to me. Roder did that. He paid attention. He didn't touch me when I didn't want him to, but when I wanted him to, there he was. And there he was, and there. *Yes.* It was astonishing, and I thought I might understand it better if we kept going like this. *Yes.* His hands felt hot and dry too, when he slid them under my shirt. My very human skin shivered and drew itself tighter as he touched me.

"You are nothing but a child molester," said Electra fiercely from the open door. Roder jerked his head up to look at her, rolling to his feet.

The thing from inside Tobiah that must have been crouching outside on the tree leapt through the window anyway, even though the android was no longer completely distracted with his back to the window. So it missed him and landed on me first, and had to scramble to get at Roder.

It tried to slide its arms under his armpits, and it wrapped its long pale legs around his middle as he rose. Roder grabbed one of its long-fingered hands and peeled it away from his shoulder, ramming the thing against the wall with his back. Electra screamed, "Help him! Where are you going? Help him!" as I ran past her, down the stairs, past Bielo who was coming up and flattened himself to let me past. There it was. I snatched my sword up from where it leaned against the wall. Fergus and Cully began to stand up as I raced out again.

When I got back, Bielo, expressionless, had the thing by the head and was bending its neck backward while Roder kept it from getting away. There was a long, rubbery crunch and then the head was dangling, but the arms and legs were still clutching Roder. Electra made a little clicking noise, half of a retch.

"Roder wasn't molesting a child, he was molesting an animal," I said to her, and her lips pulled back from her teeth as if I smelled bad.

Bielo brought his fists apart and clapped them either side of the head, which caved in. "It's dead, I think," he said.

"If it is, it's locked in position," grunted Roder. They had to break the arms and legs to loosen its grip. All the while its milky blue eyes regarded some spot in the nonexistent distance.

"What is it?" said Roder, looking at it on the floor. "Something the mages sent after me?"

"It was the thing inside Tobiah."

"What?"

"Didn't you see it? It was inside Tobiah—the witch who blew up the engine," I explained when they both looked at me. "That came out of him when he was in there."

Roder sighed. "Anything else you haven't told me?"

I shook my head. I didn't know. I knew it was a beautifully layered attack, but I didn't know if it was over yet. If Electra hadn't interrupted us, it would have worked. Any of the layers could have worked—that was the beauty of a layered strategy. If I didn't kill Roder when I first met him, if Tobiah didn't kill him on his first attack, if Zul's attack didn't work, if Tobiah didn't manage to take him out when he took out the drive—each incident led Roder to believe he was invulnerable and that he could both trust me and outfight me. Zul knew the android was a sensual being, intrigued by puzzles, and obsessed with Foresters, so he gave him a tidy little Forester puzzle package, then when the android was otherwise occupied, Tobiah made his third attack.

Had he intended another layer after this one? I didn't know. I didn't think so, but I couldn't be sure.

"Just that I am dangerous to you," I repeated, as I had said to him the night before.

He nodded and ran his fingers through his hair. "And you can't tell me just how you are dangerous. I understand," he said. It was acceptance, and it made me feel as I had when the broken engine had poured into me, but it wasn't magic and I wasn't going to get any bigger this time. If anything, I felt smaller.

"So he's your younger brother then," I said to Bielo after Roder had gone downstairs, and he gave an involuntary laugh.

"Makes me an excellent innkeeper and a lousy Monitor, having such a big need for power and control," he said, and "Come on, pretty girl," to Electra, who was still standing ramrod-straight and furious by the door. She took her eyes off me and met his level gaze with surprise. She opened her mouth, looking flustered, then he took her arm and started down the stairs before she could say anything.

It was the only comfort I had, the only assurance that I hadn't gone completely human: that I wasn't smitten with Bielo too.

CHAPTER TWENTY-THREE

Disengage (*Clammy Handshake, To Take Blades out of Engagement*)

In honor of the argument, Octavian had washed his face and combed his hair again. Pegeen had pulled a chair out from the wall and was sitting to one side, looking down over her glasses with one hard brown hand stacked on the other in her lap. It was just before dinner.

While I listened to him state his case, part of my mind was busy wondering what Pegeen and Octavian saw in each other. If I could figure that out, I could settle the puzzle I'd been meditating on all afternoon.

Octavian wasn't the puzzle. Yes, he was way past the age when the Alcibiadan agents usually threw a suicide celebration for their party favors. His bones had thickened slightly, his dark skin didn't have the tender glow it once had, and no matter how carefully he combed his hair, it wasn't silk anymore, just hair. He was still beautiful, still a living, breathing plaything, and yet, free from his agents, free to live, free to make his own choice, he chose the sarcastic dark Pegeen for his partner, and she chose him. That didn't make any sense, but then human beings didn't make sense, and I already knew that.

No, the puzzle was seated facing Octavian, leaning on his knees and listening carefully. He wasn't human, so he ought to make sense. Well, he was sort of human, modeled on a human being but designed and grown from the cell level all the way up, far too expensive for most purposes, but surely he'd been designed to make more sense than humans did.

Octavian was saying, "I do see your point. I really do. I think you need to listen to mine."

"I'm listening," said Roder.

"When I communicate with a Cybernal or an engine, I'm not just talking. My Talent isn't talking. It's more like I go inside the skin of the thing and think with it."

"Well put," muttered Pegeen austerely. He gave her a sideways glance and continued. I suspected an inside joke.

"I can only do that with magic that has a skin, some kind of a container, because otherwise I can't stay inside long enough, I slip out."

Pegeen pushed her glasses up her nose, and Octavian glanced at her again.

"Pegeen, shut up," said Roder.

Octavian continued, "That's what a Mind is. Polytechnic engineers have scooped up a certain amount of magic, and then they force the magic to make a skin for itself, a skin much smaller than it should be. It's not like a familiar, it doesn't have any real matter mixed in, it doesn't have a physical skin that holds the power in." He stopped, searching for words.

Roder waited and paid attention, though he must know all this. Everybody in the room knew it.

Bielo leaned over and said in my ear, "What's confusing you?"

I shook my head. I didn't want to ask him because he was part of the same puzzle.

Octavian said, "I know I complain a lot when you ask me to communicate, but there's a reason. Because of the way they're made, all the Cybernals, every one of them, is crazy. The Never-Mind is the worst, but they're all bad. Magic doesn't like being confined to begin with, and the skin on a Mind is too tight. They're like tortured prisoners. You can't imagine. If they weren't all so fascinating to talk to, I wouldn't do it."

"I sympathize. And what's your point?"

Octavian sighed. "That Beast down there is different. It's healthy. Somebody, some human witch, has to have made it, because magic doesn't concentrate itself like that. Whoever made it was a master, though. It's not a sealed system. It's more like a whirlpool, or a tornado, and yet it's a Mind. It's conscious. It thinks, yet it's free."

"And?"

"And it's really interesting, and it wants to talk to me, and it's not like an engine, you can go right inside it and not get burned up, and I want to go into it," finished Octavian, looking down at his hands. "That's what I do. That's my Talent."

"So we come back to what we started with," said Roder, but he was still waiting.

"Well," Octavian said, looking up at him hopefully, "it's rational, as rational as magic gets, and it's big enough to reach the Web. What if I could use it to get in touch with the NeverMind? What if I could get it to send a ship for us?"

Roder laughed. Octavian seemed to freeze, and Pegeen to turn to petrified wood, but the android leaned back and stretched. "Oh, Octavian. All right, you convinced me."

The boy relaxed. "You think it's a good idea?"

"No. It's a bad idea. You convinced me it's your own bad idea, not the Beast's. I thought you might have been taken over."

"Then I can't do it?"

"What am I, your keeper?" said Roder austerely. Now that he put it that way, I had thought he was.

"Now?"

"After dinner, for heaven's sake," said Pegeen.

We weren't in the same house anymore, or even on the same side of the city. After the Tobiah-ghost's attack, Roder and Bielo had stood together arguing quietly. Bielo had decided the encounters with the Beast and the ghost made us too conspicuous. In a discontented gaggle, we left the sunny house with the birds and slipped through the streets, invisible to spying eyes by grace of Pegeen's skill, Bear slipping along behind us. We'd seen no evidence of human beings, not even the patrolling mages who had stopped Bielo and me my first night here.

This new hiding place was a house like an explosion at a carnival. The outside was decorated with an elaborate swirling mosaic made of glass bottle bottoms, mirror pieces, buttons, dice, and small kitchen tools, but it was sedate compared to the interior. Every wall, painted and encrusted with small objects, bellied and swelled. The ceilings swooped and curled above, dribbling crystals and satin cords down to just above Cully's head.

"Don't go into the attic, it's not exactly empty," said Bielo when we came in. "Mage who owned this place incorporated himself into the decor up there a couple of years ago. He's not exactly alive anymore, but it's a little unnerving." Then he took Pegeen out to get some more food, and returned with two full coarse-woven bags. They'd walked concealed by Pegeen's skill and then bought the food openly in the market, said Bielo, because none of the vendors cared that the mages were looking for him.

Now we sat down to dinner in a large room that was an optical illusion. The walls were painted with a humid jungle scene so realistic it looked as if you could walk between the dripping boles of the nearest trees into the permanent twilight beyond. In several cases, you could, because the painting merged into sculptures of tree trunks that bordered deep alcoves set into the walls and lead nowhere. Bear was sitting on the sill of one of the alcoves, folded in around herself.

The tree branches reached to the top of the building, and the light that flickered dimly far above us was the real sky seen through the canopy of painted leaves, because the walls of this room went the whole height of the house. I had never seen trees like this on any world I'd visited, and I suspected the artist hadn't either.

We were seated at a huge stone slab the size of a boulder, encrusted with lichen and surrounded by benches that looked as if they were roughly hewn from the wood of the imaginary trees around us, eating Bielo's heavenly stew from coarse stone bowls. The decor was indeed a bit much.

"What is wrong with these people?" said Pegeen, trying to find a level spot on the boulder to balance her drinking cup, which was a glass container made to look like folded leaves. "At least the last place had flat walls and ordinary furniture, even if it was infested with conjured birds."

"This is a renegade world gone to seed," said Bielo.

"Aren't they all?" said Pegeen. "Who were the settlers?"

"I don't know. I think they ran away during the Thaumaturgic Period, after the Web was established and right around the time Enforcement got going. Five hundred years or so. After they got here, they had the usual sorcerous power struggles."

"Standard stuff?" asked Roder.

"Fire, pestilence, plague, rot, drought, mutations, the lot, from what the histories say. The witches nearly did themselves in, and I wish they had, but they were taking all the normals with them too. Sorry, present company excepted," he said when he realized why nobody else at the table was nodding. "The fighting was bad enough that they lost all their technology, magic and material alike. They were down to sympathetic magic and hoodoo spells. They pulled themselves out of it, made a magician's guild and a sort of Polytechnic, they conjured the Beast as a kind of backup filter, but they're still old-fashioned superstitious magicians, and they're loopy as drunken cats." He gestured at the room around him.

"So why are they disappearing?" said Pegeen. "Surely not a fatal addiction to interior decorating."

"They're being replaced by something else a little more sensible," said Bielo. "Mostly out in the countryside. Cottage magic, herb-lore. They don't know it yet, but most witches don't make it into the mage brotherhood anymore, they're trained at home by the herb-wives. Meanwhile, we have this grand city to maintain."

Roder's face came alive. "Could the herb-wives help us make an engine?"

Bielo laughed. "I would have told you. No, they're far too sensible to bother with big stuff. You need a mage for that."

"Can't we just stay here, Roder?" asked Electra. "It's primitive, of course, but you could change that."

Roder shook his head. "I have to find or make an engine—or get a ride out, if Octavian's Beast can send a message. I can't just give up and let Enforcement take over the Web. If Enforcement doesn't need witches anymore, you think they'll let you live?" There was silence.

"I think we're stuck here, Roder," said Fergus.

Cully said, "Bielo, how unfriendly are they to strangers in the countryside?"

"Depends," said the android. "You'd be better off looking for a home across the sea in Deistel Dom."

There was an apprehensive silence.

"Well, if we're stuck, I'm going to lose you all, aren't I?" said Roder. "It's just a matter of time."

It wasn't exactly a silence that followed. Instead, everybody decided it was time to take a sip or put a forkful in their mouths.

"Lost my crew the moment they found better jobs than the ones I could give them," said Bielo.

Pegeen said, "There aren't exactly any Forcers standing outside the door to keep us from leaving, Roder."

"I'm the last active Monitor. You are the last active crew," said Roder. "It's been over a year since I heard from any of the others. I didn't tell you that because I didn't want to put any pressure on you. But we're the only ones left to stop Enforcement."

Pegeen pushed her glasses up her nose again. Cully looked around the room.

"I'll stay with you, of course," said Electra.

There was a silence that went on too long, and she looked from face to face. Then everybody started talking at once.

CHAPTER TWENTY-FOUR

The Forward Cross Step (*Bullet Train,* To Run at Your Opponent)

After Electra began screaming at us all and ran out into the street, the discussion went back to being civilized. She returned half an hour later when it became clear nobody was going after her, least of all Roder, who seemed to take her action personally and wouldn't say a word to her for the rest of the evening. I watched from a position behind the cat in one of the alcoves. That didn't keep me completely safe. At one point, Electra turned and demanded of me, in a tone she obviously meant to sound sarcastic instead of wounded, "Well, what does the doll-baby want to do? Let's find out what she wants to do, why don't we? Are you staying with Roder or not, doll-baby?"

The cat drew its whiskers back and hissed at her. I thought that was a completely adequate response.

Bielo, who had dropped out of the discussion early, came and looked in at me in my alcove. "What was making you look so confused earlier?" he asked, ignoring the voices going on behind him.

I wasn't going to talk to him, either, but unlike Electra he seemed prepared to wait for an answer. Also unlike Electra, he could probably answer my question, even though he was just as likely to understand my motives.

"Why do they make you androids so human?" I said.

"Human? You say that like it's a dirty word."

"It's a messy word. Why do you and Roder have emotions? Why do you have to eat regular food, why do you have to sleep?"

"And?"

"And what?"

161

"And why are we made so we can fancy a pretty girl, and why did they include the equipment for dancing the old daggle-tail jig? They did, in case you were worried."

I knew I shouldn't have asked him. That last part was part of what I had been puzzled about.

"Well, early on they used to try to leave all that stuff out, and you know what happened?"

I wasn't talking to him anymore.

"Mass murderers, that's what happened. The response of a perfectly rational superhuman when faced with human behavior is homicide. We're better off irrational."

I had to agree, even though he was joking. Probably joking. The more human I became, the harder it was for me to kill. I still wasn't talking to him. He grinned and went back to watching the argument. But that wasn't my real question. My real question was, why had my master made *me* so human?

I remembered my master talking about human emotions once. "So basic, so pure," he said. "So simple when you think about it. Like any other animal. A person wants to survive. Just survive. The organism itself exists only to keep on existing. All the rest, all the technology and philosophy and social grease, all of that is only layer upon layer of elaborate justification, quite beautiful but utterly unnecessary."

My little master entertained himself in the evenings unraveling the layers of selected people he said wouldn't be missed. Sometimes he peeled away a layer or two of me when there wasn't anyone else available, but I didn't have many more layers than the dog back then so he always lost interest. Besides, he needed me.

He considered himself a perfectly rational superhuman, my little master, with his neat ringlets and his interested blue marble eyes. The room felt cold and I wrapped my arms around myself.

The discussion went in circles. "I cannot make you stay with me, and I cannot stop being a Monitor," Roder said patiently for the tenth time. "I have no choice. It's you who have to choose, but I would rather you didn't choose right away. You're assuming we are trapped here, but we haven't even tried yet. Whatever you decide to do, I am going to keep trying to contact the NeverMind and get back to the Web."

"We're on a renegade world. They don't have engines, Roder. They don't even have astronomy. We tried to hijack their Beast and it nearly ate Octavian," said Cully. Octavian frowned at him but he kept going. "Besides, what's the point? If you're the last Monitor, if Enforcement has taken over the Web, what's the point? What do we have to go back to? Enforcement doesn't need witches. Why don't you give it up?"

"You're acting as if I'm human and could choose my fate," said Roder.

Pegeen took off her glasses and squeezed the bridge of her nose, her brown fingers stiff. "You've made a lot of choices since I've known you," she said.

He smiled at her, the light eyes calm. "I was made for one thing, but I have many choices in how I go about it."

They were trying to quit their jobs and take their boss along with them, along with his reason for existing.

"Let him be," I said from the alcove and everybody jumped. They'd forgotten I existed.

"Let him be yours, you mean," said Electra, and Roder closed his eyes.

"Blessed–Spirit's–stinking–pus-stained–longjohns," said Fergus deliberately.

"I swear, Electra." Pegeen looked furious.

Electra set her mouth.

I started again, "You want to find an engine to get back in the Web. If you want, if you want, I, I can—"

"I can at least use the Beast to contact the NeverMind, for a start," interrupted Octavian, glaring at me.

"Oh, all right, all right," said Roder, laughing.

I was colder than before, shaking. I had almost done it. I had almost done it, and Octavian wouldn't let me.

"Bed," said Pegeen in a practical tone.

When everyone had left the room, Roder leaned into the alcove, pushing a sleepily complaining Bear to one side, and putting his arms under my shoulders he pulled me out. My knees were stiff.

"I appreciate your offer, whatever it was, but I will never ask you to give up your freedom," he said. "I will never ask you to be anything but what you are."

That's what I was afraid of.

He led me to the back of the house, opened the door into a dark room, and stood leaning against the jamb after I went in.

"They don't want to leave you," I said. My voice sounded muffled. There were tapestries on the walls and curtains over the window, and the room was small and very brown.

He folded his arms and leaned his head back, tired. "They will, and just as well. I give them something to do with themselves temporarily, but it's better for them to head out on their own. They don't know what it's like to have a real purpose. The first day I was squirted out of the tank, I knew what I was supposed to do with my life, and I've never done anything else. I suppose it's easier for me."

"Could you go against your nature?"

He laughed.

"Now that would be hard. Bielo managed it, so I suppose I could. I don't want to, though . . . Can I stay with you tonight?"

He watched me.

"Where is Electra?" I said.

He walked away down the hall and I heard him rummaging in the kitchen, then he returned with a wooden spoon, a plate, and something that looked like a spatula. Kneeling down and pushing the door shut, he managed to wedge the spatula and plate together under the door so that it wouldn't open easily. "There," he said. "That answer your question?"

I nodded.

There was a small rug on the floor, but he yanked the curtains out of the window and the tapestries off the walls, making me lie down and tugging and tidying the folds of fabric over me as if I were a package to be mailed or a corpse being arranged for a funeral. Shrouded, only my head peeking out, I started to giggle. "That's better," he said, and kicking his shoes off he slid into the wrappings himself. It got very hot in there, very quickly.

Yes.

In the middle of the night someone walked up to the door and tried the handle. Whoever it was, when the door wouldn't open, got down and tried to shove the untensils out from under it. I felt Roder shift position, reach out with his leg, and brace his foot against the end of the spatula, holding it in place. After a few minutes the noise stopped, but I didn't think the intruder went away for a while. Roder went back to sleep with his foot braced like that and his head tucked just above my collarbone. The cat was sleeping against my back. I don't know how she got in.

Electra looked ill in the morning, and she was ferociously polite to me all through breakfast. I wasn't sorry to leave her when Roder, Pegeen, Octavian, and I went out to try sending a message through the Beast.

Now we were outside the shabby building where the local mages kept their monster, and Octavian, trembling slightly, was murmuring under his breath, talking to the captive inside. Pegeen was looking even more egglike than usual.

"It says just come in the front door," said Octavian, leaning back on his heels with his eyes half-shut in pleasure.

"It does, does it?" said Pegeen.

He glanced at her with a half smile. She slapped him with her weathered hand, a blunt, quiet sound. It didn't look very satisfying for either of them.

He didn't move. "I am sorry," he said.

"But you're going in anyway."

"Yes."

She turned her back on him.

"Here goes," he said, stood up, and walked up the path to the unfinished wooden door. He put his hand up, it opened, and he stepped in. Pegeen closed her eyes.

We waited, crouched down. It was chilly this close to the river. A dank breeze wiped across us, and the rising pale gleam of dawn at the horizon made it feel even colder. Pegeen opened her eyes again and shoved her glasses up firmly.

"Can you tell if anything's happening?" said Roder.

"It's not my Talent," she said. "I can see what's obvious and I can hide what needs to be hidden, and that's all." She had her tight mouth even tighter and was staring at the scene before us.

The walls of the building rippled like the air above a summer road, but nothing happened.

"He likes it so much he'd risk death, and never mind me," she said, though nobody had asked.

"Well, yes," said Roder.

She shrugged and adjusted her glasses. "Forgot who I was talking to. Sounds rational to you too, doesn't it?"

A whiff of rotting mud came up from the harbor. Roder and Pegeen both wrinkled their noses. "Plenty of rustic charm here," she said.

Roder looked down at a patch of river just visible below, an olive triangle between two buildings. "They don't have much technology here, physical or magical."

"It's pathetic. This kind of thing is what Enforcement was designed to prevent, isn't it?" said Pegeen.

No, it wasn't what Enforcement was designed to prevent. This place was just a world like most human worlds, illogical, messy, and complex. Enforcement was designed to stop someone like my logical, tidy, straightforward, reasonable little master. He didn't waste energy on things like palaces and rituals, robes and spells, my master. He went right to the point. "The point, Malka, is to survive. For that, I need power, Malka. Power. Not fame, not possessions, not followers. I am no different than any other human being; my first need is to stay alive, and my second is to have power so I can stay alive comfortably."

I couldn't nod at the time, being tied to a board with some of my loose bits pinned down, but he wasn't exactly talking to me. My master's idea of survival involved moving an entire world off the Web, taking it over, and dumping his partners once they had served their purpose. His idea of surviving comfortably probably involved the slow, carefully examined death of any number of interesting people, probably starting with those partners. No, probably starting with me, once I'd stopped being useful. He had designed me to want to keep on living, after all, and nothing fascinated him more than the will to live.

Maybe that was what kept him following me all these years, instead of just making a replacement.

The back door of the Beast's building slammed open with no

notice, and I jumped to my feet. A slim figure fell out of the door, but it wasn't my master, not this time.

"Whooo!" shouted Octavian happily as Pegeen ran up to him. "Ahhh!" He got to his feet and grabbed her as she reached him, dancing her around. Two men who had been in the building behind him started toward them, and he whirled her around one more time, took her hand, and raced toward us. We all ran.

"What happened? Slow down, I think they gave up chasing us. What happened, Octavian?" demanded Roder halfway back. In the growing light Octavian's eyes were sparkling, and he was wearing a new piece of jewelry, three seamless silver rings around his neck, interwoven with the chain of his pendant.

"What didn't happen?" he replied. "It was everything I hoped."

"Did you reach the NeverMind?"

"Oh, the NeverMind knows," said Octavian. "The Never-Mind knew all along. It's all one thing. Magic's all one thing in one place. All one thing."

"Is the NeverMind sending a rescue ship?"

"You already have a rescue ship," said Octavian, smiling brightly at me.

I dropped a step behind.

"Everything's ready," he went on. "This was all meant to happen. Everything's coming to you, Roder. We don't have to decide to go anywhere. Right, Malka?"

"Oh," said Pegeen, paused, and said again, "Oh." Roder put his hand on her arm. She shook it off.

Octavian jumped up into the air from sheer joy. Pegeen followed after him, her head down.

I unfroze, joint by joint. They didn't believe him.

CHAPTER TWENTY-FIVE

The Cripple's Blow
(*Second Intention,* Pretense of Failed Attack)

It was an hour later, and Octavian still glared at us from a twisted chair in the jungle dining room. "I didn't just speak to it, I merged with it. It couldn't lie to me, I was part of it."

"Fine," said Pegeen. "You merged with magic and became one with the Web, and discovered it had a purpose and a meaning. Did you see a white light and a few dead relatives, while you were at it?"

"I didn't say I knew the meaning of the universe," said the boy. "I said magic was all one thing, and it thinks, and it has a plan."

"A cosmic plan?" said Cully carefully, fingering his beads.

"No. A backup plan. An emergency plan. A battle plan."

"You're not making sense," said Electra sternly. Fergus, his chin on his arms and his parrot shifting from foot to foot on top of his head, stared from the other side of the room. Roder stood behind him, face still.

Octavian closed his eyes and leaned back. "You don't have to believe me. But we didn't just land here by accident. We were brought here. Everything we've been looking for, it's coming here."

"We're in heaven, in other words."

"No. We're in the path of an accident about to happen. Like those Mennenkalts we were chasing after? They're coming here. We just got here ahead of them," said Octavian with irritation as if they were the ones talking vaporous nonsense.

Roder said. "Why?"

"We're in the middle of a war between Enforcement and magic," said Octavian. "The black-matter drive kills magic. Magic is fighting back." He made a sudden screaming face so graphic, so cold, so evocative of black-matter it made me shiver in agreement, but it was the final straw for the others.

"Oh, Octavian."

Octavian made a rude noise. "Soon," he said. "It's coming soon."

"Everything's falling apart. This isn't . . . it shouldn't . . . I won't have it," said Electra, and she stood up and walked out.

Bielo stood up and began to follow her.

"Stay, Bielo," said Roder. "She'll be all right. We have to plan."

Bielo kept going, Pegeen went over to Octavian and started talking to him in a lowered voice, and Fergus and Cully pushed their chairs in and left, not looking at Roder.

Roder raised an eyebrow at me. "Don't suppose you have any ideas?"

Forget it, I said, loud and messy, and the room shimmered the way the Beast's building had. Bear jumped into my lap and started kneading my thigh with her paws, staring up at me in possessive bliss. The house was silent and calm. Pegeen's face was blank, her eyes turned to the side trying to remember, Octavian's mouth drooped with disappointment in me, and Roder stared like a mannequin into space.

My master said every living thing existed only to survive, but I existed to grow louder and messier until I blew up and took my friends with me. How long did I have? Was Malka pushed or did she jump? I was full, full to bursting, and the roar of the sea pressed against the inside of my eardrums.

Something else was inside there. *"Malka?"* said Octavian from within my head. I looked up, and saw him shaking with his eyes closed, exactly as he did when he talked to the NeverMind.

"No," I answered, and he shook harder but didn't go away.

"They're coming. You have to—" he said.

Then he opened his eyes in surprise, still trembling, and said to Pegeen, "They're coming *now*. Not the Mennenkalts we were chasing, but the ones Enforcement took captive three years ago."

She looked annoyed. "What? Oh, Octavian."

Roder leaned over to put his hand on Octavian's shoulder.

"Now!" repeated Octavian in that deep wild voice, the NeverMind's voice, but in the local language. "We must defend ourselves now! Wizards, Sorcerers, Magicians, to me! Join with me!"

As he said it, he stood up. So did Pegeen, in a jerky unison, both of them startled. "Yes," said Octavian, looking at the door, and Pegeen nodded in agreement.

"Come now," said Pegeen in the local language. She looked as if she were listening to something, and when I looked at Octavian he had the same expression. They both started walking toward the door.

"Octavian," said Roder.

I leaned back, away from the door. I was in a whirlpool. Something was clawing at me.

"Octavian," repeated Roder.

Neither one answered.

"Octavian. Pegeen."

Octavian began to giggle as if somebody had told a wonderful joke, and he and Pegeen paused in the doorway, clutched each other, and laughed helplessly.

"Are you possessed?" Roder demanded. They didn't answer. In a minute, they stopped laughing, let go of each other, and started walking. He ran after them and grabbed Octavian, who didn't protest, just started trying to get loose like a cat in a net. Pegeen kept going, and Roder started after her into the street still holding Octavian.

A man in a saffron tailcoat, wearing amber jewelry and a high-domed hat, walked past without looking at them.

"I think it's something else," I said. "There's something big going on."

Roder, annoyed, was holding Pegeen by the middle, but she was walking in place. Octavian had twisted himself over so that his head stuck out from under the androids's elbow. The saffron man went past them without a glance.

"It's like holding oil with your fingers," Roder complained. "Help me." Pegeen was trying to peel his arm off her, picking away with her strong fingers. Another mage, wearing only a shirt and his neckrings, passed us without a glance.

"I'll go get Bielo," I said, and Roder nodded. But when I turned, Electra and Cully were forcing themselves past me, Cully muttering, "now" in the local language and fingering his beads. Fergus popped out after them, cheerful and oblivious with the parrot on his shoulder, but when I put a hand to his chest he walked past it. I peered into the house, and saw Bielo. He stood in the middle of the room with his hands in his trouser pockets.

"You have anything to do with the sudden urge people had to walk out on a perfectly good breakfast?" he asked me.

I looked around. Three mages in nightclothes bustled past at the end of the block, not one of them sparing me a glance. They were heading up the hill along with the current of magic, walking with the same purposeful speed as Octavian and Pegeen had. Bielo stepped into the street to stand beside Roder and stare after them. Roder was still holding Octavian, who was picking at the android's grasp and walking in place, but Pegeen had gotten away and was rounding the corner. I leaned back against the pull myself, though it wasn't pulling on me exactly. I was just a boulder in the river, not a floating leaf.

"You're not going anywhere," said Roder to me, grabbing Octavian's arm when the boy managed to worm free. "Why aren't you going with them?"

"I am not a witch," I said. "This is for witches."

"It's a spell for witches?" he said.

I nodded.

Octavian was a pretzel. He looked as if he'd willingly break a bone to get free. Roder let go. The boy began walking again and disappeared around the corner.

We started walking after them. It was still early morning, though the sun was beginning to warm the city. People forged their way past us, most of them local mages with the neck jewelry and the awful clothing. The occasional nonwitch peered from doorways and windows as we went past.

"What do you think it is? You think the boy triggered some kind of local emergency alert when he went into the Beast?" said Roder. "Is this their version of a burglar alarm?"

"Never heard of anything like it," said Bielo.

"What a mess," said Roder wearily. "I shouldn't have let him go in."

The sun shone, but I shivered. It wasn't nerves, and it wasn't cold air. It was a more familiar, bone-chilling kind of coldness, and it was somewhere near. I looked up. There was a small orange speck, a ball, in the sky above the harbor, and that was where the coldness was coming from.

"Octavian didn't set it off. I know what the emergency is," I said. "He was right. Enforcement's here."

Roder laughed.

"Really," I said, and pointed. He peered along the line of my finger and raised his eyebrows, watching it approach.

I craned my neck and the Enforcement ship was close enough to see now. It was an old sanction transport, a refit, not one of their new little bulbous arrows, and it was meant to spend long periods in open space and free fall. The orange skin of the ship was broken at intervals by hatches, portholes, access bays, and patches where the skin had worn away and been replaced by other material. The drive end was aimed toward us, like an axle, keeping still while the rest of the ship revolved. In the center of it was the viewing port of an iris door in the center of that. Around the axle, the words *Hilma K. Lewis* revolved, around and around, and it gave off an aura of bitter cold.

Class Three sanction on Mennenkaltenei, three years ago. Twelve thousand Mennenkalts aboard the *Hilma K. Lewis*. Last heard off the Web chasing an escaped prisoner. We might be off the Web, but we hadn't escaped.

"That's the emergency, then," said Roder. Bielo nodded. They both sighed in unison. "Too bad," said Roder. "We're dead."

There was a huge surge in the flow of magic up the hill, and the people passing us began to run full speed. The whole world seemed to pause, and a dark column of smoke rose above the center of the city, a twisting shape like the body of a tornado. It loomed over us.

In the pause, in the stillness, the column of smoke took on the form of a giant. It had a head, and arms, and enormous legs. It reached back with one incredibly long arm and made a throwing motion that seemed to last forever and to cover the whole sky.

Then it finished the throw, and the world began to move again.

Several small things shot out of the iris door of the Enforcement ship and fell, and at the same time the axle slowly began to turn along with the rest of the craft. The ship too fell, for one breathless second, as if it were going to crack like an egg on the city below. Then the spinning sphere halted in midair, took a sprightly hop, and after a single swooping pass to the hills north of the city it landed like a bird.

Roder stood with his mouth open. "They did it," he said. "That's not normal flight. The locals did it."

"They can't have," said Bielo. "Enforcement engines are impervious to spells. They can't have."

Silence. They both stared.

"Now we're really in trouble," said Bielo, and Roder nodded.

People were still walking up and heading blindly toward the top of the hill, and magic was still pouring past me.

The twisting column of smoke above the center of the city folded in half and vanished like dust in the wind.

There was a blinding fountain of magic pouring back down the hill. I heard far-off yelling, and two people who had just passed us going up turned around in bewilderment, stared at each other, and began to run back down the hill. More people began running past us, though others were walking and talking.

"We're in for it," said Roder. "They're sure to notice us."

"No," said Bielo and chuckled. "They won't notice a thing. I'll bet they're all holding their bowels shut with knees and elbows right now."

A man in gray and blue stripes, as if to contradict Bielo,

glanced at me. *Not here, not now.* His legs buckled and he sat down. Too loud. I couldn't control it anymore. But at least he forgot me as he staggered back to his feet and ran on. Roder and Bielo hadn't noticed. We kept going up the hill against the flow.

When we reached the square at the top, it was almost empty. All the witches had scattered, and Octavian and Pegeen, with their arms around each other, were walking toward us. There were two natives likewise embracing in the small garden at the center, a bald man and a long-haired woman, and beyond them in the red building the sound of many voices raised in far-off fury.

"I told you," said Octavian severely as he and Pegeen came close enough to be heard.

"You told me, Octavian," said Roder. "You were right."

"Hah. Kaihan's back in town. I should have known," said Bielo, not listening to them. He pointed.

"What?"

"The bald man over there. He's the mage I told you about. The local witch who might be able to build you a drive. The one who might be willing to do it."

Maybe I was safe after all.

"Who's that?" said the bald man when Bielo called his name. He shaded his eyes against the early-morning sun. The black-haired woman he was embracing turned to face us too. She saw me, and I saw what she was in the same moment.

Maybe I wasn't safe after all.

Octavian had been right. It was all happening at once, and all in the same place. I started backing away.

"Ekestverte yer andanfellter, lle perfent kamm!" she started in amazement, her insane green eyes widening. "Lle kurfurst? Lle kurfurst zhatter?" The power glowed from her. She was speaking directly to me, directly to the ocean inside me. She saw me. She saw all of me.

"*NO,*" I said, still backing away. "Thank you, *no.* I like it this way." We had found the escaped prisoner the *Hilma K.* had been chasing. She was a Mennenkalt, but worse, she was one of the Mennenkalt gods, one of the ones they bred for the Power. I could smell it, glowing from her like a loaf fresh from the oven.

Like every other Mennenkalt I met, she wanted to break me open like a penny bank, and unlike every other one I'd met she could do it without my permission.

CHAPTER TWENTY-SIX

The Counterattack
(*Screaming Geek*, Against
Attack Already in Progress)

We were inside the black tower, the ugly tall one on the square with the blue lights coming out of the top. It was just as ugly inside, and even darker, and it belonged to the imperious bald gentleman, Kaihan, who sat cross-legged on the floor as if he were above us on a throne. He was listening to Roder, had been listening to him for ten minutes without saying anything and without moving. In spite of his torn and grubby shirt, in spite of the long red scratch and the scum of grime on his face, in spite of the weariness that gave a squint to the hard black eyes, he was almost as frightening a character as his girlfriend, for the power in him was like a knife.

Bielo was right. The natives couldn't have downed the Enforcement transport without somebody like this. The other local witches had all been merely people with a little Talent. This man was an elemental, more of a spirit than a human witch.

The reason I was sitting as far from the others as I could wasn't the powerful Kaihan, though. The reason I had my back to the wall and an eye on the door was squatting on her haunches beside him, rebraiding her long hair. She was almost as dirty as he was, as if the two of them had been rolling around on the ground. I didn't trust her, even if she *had* apologized.

I didn't trust her because every time she looked at me, and she looked at me often, her pupils contracted as if she were looking at the sun. She wasn't trying to crack me open anymore, but I was making her ill, and that was quite an accomplishment. She was one of the highest of the human deities of the Mennenkalts. Kaihan called her "Lisane," which was a Mennenkalt word, but he obviously didn't know what it meant.

It meant "nameless," the same way the Hom Bulos called magic "RGWG the Unnamable."

Roder stopped talking. Neither of our new acquaintances jumped in to fill the silence. Kaihan's black eyes didn't waver. He was as much like the other mages I'd seen as an alligator was like a poodle.

"Please—" Electra started, and Bielo put his hand over her mouth. She had been crouching on the porch of the white building and ran to Roder when we reappeared, but Bielo had intercepted her then, too. Pegeen, cloaked, had gone out to find where Fergus and Cully were.

The man didn't move. I wasn't even sure he was breathing. In the last half hour Roder had given him a brief history of the Web and of the technical development of witchcraft, explained what Enforcement was, outlined the job of Monitor, laid out the present situation, and asked him if he would consider making us an engine, while giving him a crash course in cosmology that had some rather large holes. Kaihan's only question so far had been one about how stars made their light, which he quickly retracted with an apology for wasting time.

Now he said in his deep voice, "Instantaneous travel and speech over vast distance?"

Roder nodded.

"And these Enforcers of yours, when their control is even slightly threatened, they retaliate immediately by destroying whole worlds."

"Lately, yes, they have been."

He still didn't move. Austere bugger. "I have no idea how to make this thing you want."

"Well, I do," said the nameless Mennenkalt goddess, and my stomach clenched, but she continued: "I made a little one when I ran away."

She made it sound trivial. She had gotten herself off an interstellar transport in midtranslation, all by herself. She had escaped a platoon of Enforcers, all by herself. She had stolen a little rocket lifeboat and made an engine all by herself, and landed on a strange planet, and made nice with the most powerful magician around, all by herself. The Mennenkalt gods were fearsome creatures.

"Ah, yes," said Kaihan, regarding her.

She tucked her black hair behind her ear.

He turned back to Roder. "If I make you one and let you go away, can you keep them from destroying us all after you're gone?" said Kaihan. "Ah. I see that's the question. These Enforcers will kill us, won't they? No matter what we do."

The inside of this tower was a sink of silence. When nobody was moving or speaking, you couldn't hear anything at all except a kind of deep heaviness in the air.

Roder sighed, finally. "If you had enough power and enough magic and enough time, you could make an engine big enough to move the whole world. I knew of a man who did it once."

I wasn't going to say anything. Wasn't going to volunteer, if there were a chance, if there was any other way. The woman stared at me as if she could see what I was thinking. Her pupils were tiny holes in the green sea of her eyes.

"But we do not have enough time," said Kaihan.

"Time is relative. Time is just an idea. We have enough power, and we have enough magic," said Lisane.

I pressed my back against the wall, hard, feeling the rough coldness of the black stone against my shoulder blades. *No.*

Everybody flinched. "Would you just stop that, child? You're hurting everybody," said Electra. She turned her face against Bielo's hand.

"Child?" said Lisane. "She's as old as the ages, as big as the sky, and she knows what's good for her, which is more than I can say for you. No, spirit of anger," she said to me respectfully in Mennenkalt, "I do not question thy will or thy vision, and I will seek thy help elsewhere." Once again, she seemed to be talking to all of me, in a spooky way.

She stood up. "You want to try?" she said to Kaihan.

He regarded her with those cold black eyes, not looking any more convinced than he had a moment before. "Why do you even ask me?" he said. "You will do as you wish." She leaned down, said something in his ear, and strode to the front door. He watched her go, and there was a crease at the corner of his mouth that told me the basilisk was smiling.

"Then we must make a world engine, not a little boat that will hold only you," he said to Roder, and that was that. He was no trusting savage. He knew what was involved. It took tremendous arrogance to make such a decision for a whole world.

Roder took it for the ultimatum it was, though Electra, looking from face to face, was ready to jump in and fight until Bielo took her off to one side and talked face-to-face for a long time. By the time he was done, she was looking as complacent as ever, especially after he kissed her hand.

Outside Kaihan's coal-colored tower the rest of the country was going to hell in a number of creative ways, Pegeen reported when she came back with the others. The moment the transport ship landed, all its prisoners poured out and began to settle in, causing interesting interactions with the natives. Some of the refugees, determined to straighten things out, had already reached the fringes of the city. Mennenkalts were peaceful people, but opinionated and persistent, and there were twelve thousand of them.

Meanwhile, the local government was too wounded to cope. The creation of the spell had required the power of all the witches in the world, most of whom had not been volunteers, and the resulting quarrels were fierce.

Kaihan listened to this with his hand over his eyes and decided to ignore the political turmoil his world was in. He called in a colleague to help, a surly gentleman with a long white beard by the name of Gelmas who looked vaguely familiar to me, and I puzzled over that until I realized he'd been the elderly gent with the prisoner and the horse the day before. While Kaihan explained things to his annoyed friend, Lisane stood in the doorway and spoke in Mennenkalt to the air outside, saying things that made my insides crawl.

Fergus said, "She's sending out an invitation to a party?" I'd forgotten how poorly he understood Mennenkalt.

Cully answered patiently, "The pronoun makes a difference, Fergus."

Then endless rivers of magic began surging in, flooding the

chamber. The others looked as pale and ill as when they were in translation. I, on the other hand, grew hot, dizzy, and replete.

After that, creating a living drive seemed to require much arguing and plenty of chalk. Kaihan's friend Master Gelmas was squatting in his white robes scribing geometric shapes on Kaihan's clean black floor. "It's not just the motion of the wandering stars which must be taken into account," he said authoritatively, drawing a precise arc between two of the points of a nine-pointed star. "The fixed stars have a proper motion as well."

Kaihan perched on the bottom step of his black throne rubbing his shoulders. He's wiped his face clean and changed into austere black clothing. "Balderdash," he said. "The fixed stars haven't got a thing to do with it. This fellow says they're big suns and not even close to one another."

"You can't deny that my methods work," said the other man, picking up a different color and drawing a straight line by putting the chalk to the floor and shuffling backward.

"Your methods work because they amuse the spirits," said the Lisane, standing in the doorway. "I find them pretty funny myself." Glemas glared at her.

"It's just the . . . genetics . . . of . . . brain chemistry," said Fergus, using Standard words for half the sentence because there weren't any words in the local language.

"Just the gobbledygook?" mocked Master Gelmas, not understanding most of what Fergus had said. "Is that all?"

Fergus rolled his eyes, and groped for words. "People are either born with brains that can interact with magic, or they're not. Spells are just a way of focusing the mind. They're no necessary."

Master Gelmas finished the line with a neatly drawn interlocking knot. "Of course. That's obvious. But without carefully crafted spells, you don't have focus and all you get is nonsense." He went back to the center and started drawing another straight line in a third color. The line passed under Kaihan' feet, which he lifted up while the old man shuffled past.

I watched from one of the stairways that wound up the inside of Kaihan's vast tower while they moved around and squabbled. The room was bulging with magic. The heated pressure wa steady, pushing on all of me, burying my outer layers, but it wasn't unpleasant, and it wasn't just caused by Lisane's be-speaking or the scribblings of Master Gelmas. Somehow or an-other, Roder's witches, the Lisane, and the local mages were weaving something intricate together. Master Gelmas created an interlocking diagram that covered the whole circular floor, around the nine-pointed star in the center. Octavian straddled it, his black-fringed eyes half-closed. He still seemed elated from his morning's encounter with the Beast, though he wouldn't say anything about it and he wouldn't look at me. "The flow in the north is weak," he would say with a smile, and Pegeen would walk to that end of the diagram and stare at the floor. Fergus, following her, would stoop when she pointed and draw patterns in the air with his fingers.

With each layer Master Gelmas scribed, Kaihan moved a step higher on his throne, occasionally holding his broad hands out as if warming himself at a fire. The Lisane walked and watched, moving from one end of the diagram to another, talk-ing and talking, seeing things none of the rest of us could see, staring at me from time to time, and her face was the color of skim milk.

Just outside the design, Cully and Electra stood against op-posite walls, Cully sliding beads through his fingers and Electra fluttering her hands over her small animal, and every once in a while one of them would say something quiet to another one of the participants. Only Roder and I had nothing to do. The air was heavy and hot, and I was restless and confused, but the oth-ers seemed unaffected by the heat so I said nothing.

"Have you thought what form it should take?" inquired Kai-han. "Animal? Human? Abstract?"

"It will take what form it happens to take," grunted the old man, holding the front of his robe bunched in one hand so he wouldn't sweep out the marks he was making with the other hand. "If we had time to make this a year-project I would bother with aesthetics."

The Lisane stopped, balancing on one foot. "Not aesthetics. Function follows form. The tool shapes the task."

"Crude sympathetic magic," said Electra in Standard to Cully.

"I guess they believe the charm should look like the thing it's supposed to affect."

The Lisane caught the condescending tone, if not the meaning. "I am talking about the natural form of a being. Things are true to their natures, and form is part of nature."

"Wouldn't human be easiest?" Kaihan moved another step upward.

"No. Human form is the most difficult and the most dangerous." She met my eyes and balanced on the other foot. "When you make a living thing, it should be like enough to you that you can speak with it, but unlike enough that you don't expect to understand it. Unless you have a compelling reason otherwise." She hopped to the next open space.

"Only the novice speaks of what should be, not what is," muttered Gelmas.

Electra wasn't convinced. In Standard, she said to Cully, "Why does it have to have a shape at all? Drives don't have a shape, minds don't have a shape. Seems to me these primitives are making a lot of fuss over window dressing."

"It's good basic engineering, and you're being rude," said Pegeen acerbically from across the room. "Why do you think every witch's familiar has a different shape? It's not just because they feel like it."

Electra rolled her eyes.

"It's lopsided again on that side," called Octavian to Pegeen, waving toward our end of the hall.

Somebody hammered on Kaihan's door. He ignored it.

"Still lopsided," called Octavian.

Fergus sat back on his heels. "I've retied this intersection three times already. What's going on?"

"I don't know. It feels like the floor's on a slant and everything's rolling downhill."

The hammering came again. "Somebody please get that," said Kaihan.

I stepped where Roder did, in between the lines, carefully skipping the blank spots he skipped. Master Gelmas had a hand that was supernaturally steady. The lines looked as if they had been ruled, or grown, or poured across the floor from an enor-